The Man with No Past

In the wilds of Arizona a man wakes up to find that not only does he have a nasty head wound, but amnesia as well. Unaware of who he is, or even where he is, all he has to go on is a name in a bible in the saddlebags of a lame horse grazing nearby. The name is Zachariah Thompson, and an inscription inside the bible says it was presented to him by the grateful citizens of Helena in Montana.

Believing himself to be this man, he carries on his way, eventually collapsing and being found unconscious by a rancher and his daughter who nurse him back to health. But when the ranch is attacked by an Apache band, the father is killed, leaving Zach and the rancher's daughter to flee for their lives.

But Zach begins to question his identity when he is mistaken for a notorious outlaw....

The Man with No Past

Pete B. Jenkins

A Black Horse Western

ROBERT HALE

© Pete B. Jenkins 2020
First published in Great Britain in 2020

ISBN 978-0-7198-3120-1

The Crowood Press
The Stable Block
Crowood Lane
Ramsbury
Marlborough
Wiltshire SN8 2HR

www.bhwesterns.com

Robert Hale is an imprint
of The Crowood Press

*For Serena Alethea Gay Jenkins (née Downs) my precious wife.
I still love you deeply even after all these years together.*

Typeset by
Simon and Sons ITES Services Pvt Ltd
Printed and bound in Great Britain by
4Bind Ltd, Stevenage, SG1 2XT

ONE

He knew something terrible had happened as soon as he opened his eyes and found himself lying on his back. His body hurt all over, and as his hand went up to probe his head he discovered his dark hair matted with dry blood. With difficulty he rolled over, and getting to his knees, took in his surroundings.

A mare stood ten yards or so away, her head down and grazing contentedly on the rough grass that grew in tufts here and there amongst the rocky terrain. She was fully saddled, her reins dragging across the stony ground as she took a few steps forwards to get to the next bunch of grass.

He had no idea where he was, how he had got here, or even what had happened to him. Dang it, he couldn't even remember who he was.

The fact that the wound on his head sported dried blood told him he had been unconscious for a while. The gash across the top of his skull must have pumped out blood steadily for quite some time before it coagulated, and then taken several hours more to actually crust over.

He figured he may have been lying there for the better part of twenty-four hours before he came round.

He was thirsty. He was beyond thirsty, and it was no small wonder. The sun was beating down hot and strong, and he had no idea when he had last tasted water. Shakily getting to his feet he staggered over to the mare, and lifting the canteen from the saddle horn, was relieved to discover it was half full. Pulling the cork he drank deep of the lukewarm water.

'Where are we, girl?' he said to the mare, who lifted her head to peer round at him momentarily before going back to the more important business of filling her belly.

For miles in every direction all he could see was rocks and dirt with an occasional stunted tree, and those brown tufts of grass that the horse was so interested in. It was a barren place, that was for sure.

As his attention strayed from his surroundings back to the mare he noticed she was hobbling slightly – yep, she was definitely favouring her left hind leg. His heart sank, of all the rotten luck. It would be a day or two before she would be able to take a man on her back, and that meant he had a very long walk ahead of him, something that he didn't relish, given the state he was in himself.

His head was throbbing now that he had stood up, and it got him to thinking about how it had happened. Maybe the mare had stepped in a hole and hurt her leg, which had caused her to throw him. It wasn't too much of a stretch of the imagination to believe he could have struck his head against one of the many rocks strewn about, although he couldn't see any one in particular that revealed a smattering of blood. It was really the only explanation he could come up with, given that his mind was in such a muddle.

As he hooked the canteen back over the saddle horn his eyes fell on the saddlebags, and it gave him the idea that the answer to his identity might be contained within those leather bags; so eagerly lifting the flap of the first one, he rummaged around inside.

Pulling out a dog-eared leather-bound book, he turned it over to see what it was, and didn't feel at all surprised to discover it was a bible. Flipping it open he read the inscription aloud: *'This bible presented to Zachariah Thompson for services rendered to the citizens of Helena, 1878.'* The only Helena he knew of was in Montana. Glancing about, he sighed: this was definitely not Montana. There was nothing else written in that bible, and so closing it, he carefully placed it back in the saddlebag.

Well, that was it, then. His name must be Zachariah Thompson. Opening the other saddlebag he rummaged around in much the same fashion as he had the first one, discovering nothing more than a few hard biscuits, a couple of dollars in coins, and a worn Colt .44 with a half empty box of shells. All he had was a name, but nothing else that would tell him what his occupation was, nor where he had been heading to. It was going to be a case of walking out of this semi-desert until he came to a town, and by then maybe his memory would have come back to him.

'Come on, girl,' he said, as he gathered up the mare's reins. 'We've got a long, hot walk ahead, but I reckon between the two of us we'll make it.'

Two days later a small group of buildings loomed on the horizon, and Zachariah offered up a little prayer of thanks. His water had run out earlier in the day, and the mare hadn't had anything to drink since before Zach had come round from his accident, so she was in about as bad a state as she could be and still be alive.

Placing one foot after another he doggedly crossed the ground until he found himself plodding wearily up the short dusty street of the little hamlet, his eyes riveted to the largest building that had 'saloon' emblazoned above its plate glass window; he didn't stop until his mare had her head down in the horse trough in front, greedily gulping down great drafts of the stagnant water.

'Dang it, mister, you look as if you're about done in,' the whiskery bartender said as Zach sidled up to the bar to order a beer.

'I feel about done in, too,' Zach admitted, as he pulled a few coins out of his pocket and slapped them down on the rough-hewn countertop.

'When was the last time you ate?' the whiskery fellow asked, his eyes taking in Zach's hair, which was still caked with dried blood.

Zach shook his head. 'I don't remember, unless you can count two hard-tack biscuits I had a few days back as food.'

'I've got some stew cooking in a pot out back, so how about I get you a bowl? That and the whiskey won't cost you more than two bits.'

'Sounds good.'

'So where is it you're heading to, mister?' the bartender asked when he came back with a steaming bowl of stew and placed it in front of Zach.

'Nowhere in particular,' he answered. It was the truth, really; he didn't have a clue where he had been heading before he had the accident.

'Well, you'll find plenty of places like that here in Arizona,' the man said, and then chuckled slightly.

So this was Arizona. Zach had entertained a sneaking suspicion it might be, given that the countryside was so arid. So now he knew his name was Zachariah Thompson and that he was in Arizona. Given another week he just might figure out what he was supposed to be doing here.

'I 'spect you could do with a bath, too.'

'A bath and a bed, if there's one going.'

The bartender looked pleased. 'There sure is. Give me an hour and I'll have your bath ready for you. You'll find your room at the top of the stairs. It's the second door on the left.'

Zach nodded. He looked forward to sleeping in a real bed at last, instead of out there on that stony ground he had been subjected to for the past few days. Maybe a good hot bath and a restful night's sleep would be enough to restore his memory to him, and the good Lord knew how important that was if he was going to get his life back in order.

He felt a new man after the bath, but when he woke up the next morning, despite having had a wonderful sleep, he was still no closer to knowing anything about himself. That clonk to the head had really done a job on him, and for the first time since he had woken up out there on that hard dry ground he began to fear his memory would never come back to him.

'Will you be leaving today, mister?' the bartender asked him, as he placed a plate laden with bacon and eggs in front of him later on that morning.

'I think I'll stay on another day to give my mare a chance to recover,' Zach said, 'but I'll head off after that,' although he really had no idea where he would be heading to.

'Well, if you're ever back this way you be sure to stop off and I'll have a bath, warm bed, and a hot meal ready for you.'

Zach didn't think he ever would be back, but he nodded his head and managed a smile for the fellow's benefit anyway. Wherever he had been heading to, it had to be better than this broken down little town, its buildings coated thickly with the red dust that the wind regularly whipped up and blew through the place. He rested up for the rest of that day and then slept like a baby that night. The next morning he headed down to the livery and was pleased to discover that the mare's hind leg was back to rights again – obviously all she had needed was the weight taken off it for a day or so.

Zach headed off with some vague directions as to how to get to Wickenburg, a small town a few days' ride from where he was at the moment, and he hoped that by the time he reached it, the reasons why he had come to this part of the country would come back to him. Surely the memory loss he was suffering couldn't be permanent – his past would come back to him soon enough, and he would remember what he did for a living, and why he was in Arizona.

A day out and his head began to trouble him. He really should have laid up for a few more days before he lit out for Wickenburg, given that he had suffered a nasty blow to his skull that must have rattled his brains as well as his teeth. You don't just spring back from an injury like that in a matter of a couple of days. The problem was, he was starting to see two of everything, and he knew dang well that they weren't doubling up on him, so it had to mean he was experiencing some sort of delayed reaction from the head wound. He still had a day to go before he reached Wickenburg, so if things got worse where his eyesight was concerned, then he might just find himself in a whole heap of trouble.

Six hours later Zach knew for sure that he was in trouble. His balance was such that he was having difficulty staying in the saddle, and he had begun to sweat more than was normal for the conditions he was travelling under. He wasn't going to make it to Wickenburg after all: in fact it looked like he was going to die out here, miles away from anybody, his body left for the wild animals to feast upon, and then his bones bleached by the hot Arizona sun.

He was getting drowsy now, consciousness was rapidly slipping away from him, and he knew it would only be a matter of a few minutes before he slipped from the saddle and came to rest on the hard ground beneath his mare's feet. The last thought he had before he felt himself go was that he hoped his death would be a quick one, and that he wouldn't linger for days before thirst, or hunger or wild animals took him from this world into the next.

TWO

Zach's eyes suddenly opened. He was lying flat on his back, but it wasn't the Arizona sky he was staring up at – above his head was a wooden ceiling painted in pale blue.

'Pa … Pa, you'd best come in here!'

The sweet female voice had come from somewhere to the left of where he lay, and so Zach did his best to turn his head in that direction. Before he could pick out the speaker a door had been flung open and he heard the sound of heavy footsteps crossing the floor. A man with silvery hair suddenly peered down at him with a look of concern on his face.

'How are you feelin', lad?' he asked gently.

Zach's head was pounding, despite the fact he was comfortably positioned on a soft mattress. 'I've felt better,' he admitted.

'I found you out there 'bout three miles from the house. Thought you was dead at first!'

It was all coming back to Zach now. He had lost consciousness and fallen from his mare. He was surprised he was still alive. But then, he figured he owed the fellow staring down at him for that.

'Was two days back that I found you,' the older man continued. 'Don't know how long you'd been there for, but your horse was near done in from lack of water. It was all I could do to lead her back here.'

'Is she …?'

'She's just fine, lad, so don't you worry 'bout her. I've got her runnin' free out back of the house where there's plenty of grass and water.'

Zach's eyes were working overtime to try and locate the owner of that feminine voice he had heard a few minutes back, and those eyes weren't disappointed when they finally came to rest on her. She was standing over by a dresser, her long, wavy hair shining like cornsilk in the sun that streamed in through the open window.

The old man caught sight of the look on Zach's face and chuckled. 'Come here, Emily, I think our guest wants to get a closer look at you.'

The girl did as she was told, and standing beside the bed gave Zach his first unimpeded look at her.

'She's a beauty, ain't she, son?'

Zach didn't answer: he was just too tongue-tied to try. The young woman standing over him was beyond beautiful. It was as if the Creator had decided to fashion a creature that would put the angels to shame, and so had come up with what Zach was seeing now. She was lovely beyond belief – a rare jewel amongst even the prettiest of women, and Zach could feel his poor heart beginning to beat faster

13

in his breast, a testament to the fact that despite his sorry physical condition he could still work up plenty of enthusiasm for the fairer sex.

'Emmy's the one that's been lookin' after you for the past couple of days,' the girl's father confessed. 'I reckon you couldn't have a better nurse than her.'

Zach's dark brown eyes made contact with Emily's vividly green ones. 'Thank you,' he croaked, his throat dry from lack of water.

'You're welcome,' she said sincerely. 'Now that you're awake I'll fix you something to eat and drink,' and then she disappeared before he had a chance to reply.

Pulling up a chair the girl's father sat down close to the bed. 'I took the liberty of checkin' through your saddlebags before I brought you back here. Just to make sure you weren't hidin' somethin' you shouldn't be,' he confessed.

'Worried I was on the run from the law?'

The fellow chuckled. 'A feller can't be too careful these days. Arizona seems to attract more'n its fair share of desperate hombres. I can do without one of 'em in my house, especially with Emily bein' here.' He tilted his head slightly to one side as if he was trying to make Zach out. 'I take it from the inscription inside your bible that your name is Zachariah Thompson?'

'I reckon it is,' Zach conceded.

'I figure a man what gets given a bible by an entire town for renderin' service to 'em can't be too bad a feller.'

'I like to think so.'

14

'Doesn't explain why you're way out here, though. Nor why I found you near dead with that head wound.'

'I wish I knew myself, but I'm afraid I can't remember much of anything.'

'You tellin' me you've lost your memory?'

'That's about the size of it.'

'Well glory be, if'n that don't beat all.'

'I can't remember anything beyond a few days back.'

'Not even why you're here in Arizona?'

'Nope, not even that. All I know is my name is Zachariah Thompson.'

'Glory be!' the old fellow said again, only with more emphasis this time, 'you're a man without a past.'

Zach's head was beginning to clear now. 'I must thank you for your kindness,' he said with sincerity. 'I reckon I'd be dead by now if you hadn't happened upon me and brought me here.'

The old man waved the comment away. 'Couldn't leave a feller out there in that blisterin' sun to die like a dog, an' I'm sure you would've done the same for me if'n the roles was reversed.'

Zach wasn't sure what he would have done. He had no idea what kind of a man he was, for that matter. All he had to go on was what was written in that bible, and that seemed to say he was a man held in high esteem, by the good folks of Helena at least.

'You're welcome to stay here for just as long as you need to. I figure it'll take several days before you're back to rights and able to straddle that mare of yours, anyhow.'

15

'I'm much obliged to you …?'

'Jeff … Jeff Fawcett.'

Zach nodded: 'Well, thank you, Jeff, for everything.'

'Don't mention it.' Getting to his feet, Jeff looked down at the youngster for a moment. 'I'll leave you to rest up now. I reckon Emily'll be back in here in a while with some food and drink. That'll soon put some strength back into your body for you.'

Zach watched him as he headed for the door, a tall statuesque sort of a man, who commanded respect just by his mere presence. Zach had no doubt he was in safe hands, and would be back on his feet in no time.

Emily returned about ten minutes later with a tray of food and a pot of steaming hot coffee. Placing it down on the chest of drawers beside the bed she helped Zach to sit up, and then placed a couple of pillows behind him to keep him in the sitting position.

'Hopefully, it will only be a day or so before you're well enough to sit at the table and eat your meals with Pa and me.'

'I'd like that very much.'

She smiled at him then, and if she had been beautiful before, then she took her appeal to a whole other level when her face lit up the way it did. If he wasn't careful he was going to end up falling in love with this young woman, and never wanting to leave.

After placing the tray of food on his lap she sat down in the chair her father had vacated and watched him eat. 'I hope Pa hasn't been asking you too many questions about yourself,' she said eventually.

'He's been remarkably restrained. I think if it had been me who'd taken in a wounded stranger I'd want to know as much about him as I possibly could, especially if he was going to be spending time under the same roof as my beautiful daughter.' He wasn't sure why he had added that last bit, but it just seemed to slip out of him.

Emily Fawcett blushed, her pale skin going a deep crimson. She obviously wasn't used to men paying her compliments. He pretended he hadn't noticed so as not to cause her any more discomfort than he already had.

'I take it this is a ranch I'm on,' he said, being careful not to look at her, but to concentrate on the food on his plate instead, so as to give her time for her visible embarrassment to subside.

'Yes, it is. It isn't good land but there's only Pa and me to support, so we do well enough. That's as long as the renegade Apache leave us alone. They've run off quite a few head of cattle as well as horses in the past few years.'

'That'd be Geronimo and his band, I suspect.'

'That's what Pa thinks, too.'

'He's a problem is that one. Many a man has tried to hunt him down, but he's as elusive as a ghost. I think it'd take one of his own people to bring him to light.'

'Will you be heading on to Wickenburg when you're better?'

He looked at her now and fancied he saw sadness in her eyes, and figured it was because living out here she didn't get to see too many people, so when she did, she found it hard to let go of them.

'I expect so,' he confessed. 'After that I might just head on to Tombstone.'

She screwed her face up at his mention of the place. 'Pa and I have heard bad things about that town.'

'So have I, but I've also heard there are employment opportunities as well.'

'Usually of the baser sort, I'm afraid.'

Zach figured the girl was merely going on hearsay. What could she possibly know about Tombstone, living way out here in the wilds of Arizona? The truth was, Tombstone was a town of opportunity, and seeing as he had no dang idea who he was or even what skills he had, trying his luck in Tombstone seemed like a mighty good idea, rough town or not.

'Pa tells me you can't remember anything beyond a few days back.'

'I'm afraid not. I remember waking up on the ground and making it to a small town, if you can call it that, and laying up there for a couple of days. But I remember nothing at all of my life before that.'

'That must be frightening for you.'

'I wouldn't recommend it to anyone, that's for sure,' Zach agreed.

'You must have family that will be worried about you.'

That thought hadn't entered Zach's head until now. Maybe there was someone out there waiting for him to turn up who would be concerned that he hadn't. Maybe they would come looking for him. If they did, and found him, then they could give him the answers to the questions he so badly wanted to know.

'You must have family somewhere, Zach,' Emily said when he didn't answer.

'I guess I do,' he conceded, 'but I just don't remember.'

He was beginning to wonder if he was ever going to regain any knowledge of his past. Maybe those memories were gone forever. Just maybe that knock he had received had permanently damaged the part of his brain that allowed a man to recall his life and all that he had done. It was as if his life hadn't started until that moment he had woken up on the ground a few days back. Everything else was just a complete blank. He didn't know what he was good at, what he liked or disliked, or even what company he usually kept. His fear was he would have to learn almost everything all over again, and that would place him at a definite disadvantage.

After he had finished eating and Emily had taken his plate and cup away, Zach slipped back under the covers and considered his future. His hands looked too soft for him to be a working man, but the clothes he had been wearing didn't label him as the sort who worked in a store or behind a desk, either. What his line of work was presented a mystery, that was for sure, a mystery he figured he was going to need to solve real quick if he wanted to survive.

THREE

Zach was up and around five days later, and eager to earn his keep. He helped Jeff split firewood for the better part of a day to keep Emily's stove in fuel for the next few weeks, and was just stacking an armload of the stuff beside the stove when he heard voices back out in the yard, and by the sounds of it they were all male.

Straightening up, he walked over to the window and peeped out. Jeff Fawcett was standing with hands by his side and fists curled up tightly as he confronted two men on horseback. Emily was standing behind her pa, the washing basket full of wet clothes she had carried out to the line to hang up still in her hands. She looked frightened.

Zach sized up the situation. The two men looked to be of the rougher type. Unshaven and uncouth in appearance, they kept leering at Emily as her father remonstrated with them. It wasn't hard to see what their intentions were, and unfortunately, although Jeff was out there without a gun, both saddle tramps were packing shooting irons.

Zach weighed up his options. These men were planning to take Emily against her will, and being unarmed, Jeff wouldn't be able to stop them. Most likely they would put a bullet in him first to make things easier where Emily was concerned, and probably do the same to her once they had finished with her. He had to do something, and he had to do it now. Walking through to the bedroom he pulled the old Colt .44 with its holster from his saddlebags and strapped it on. Maybe if he stepped out on to the porch and they saw he was armed they might back off. With his heart thumping away in his chest he retraced his footsteps to the front door, and then opening it up stepped outside to an uncertain fate.

The two men were too engrossed in what they were doing to notice Zach's presence.

'How about it, sweetheart,' one man was saying to Emily, 'you want to go into the barn with Frank and me for a roll in the hay?'

'Don't you speak to my daughter like that, you scum!' Jeff barked angrily.

'Or what old man ... you gunna teach me and Frank a lesson?'

'If need be,' Jeff answered bravely, even though he knew either man could pull iron on him any time they wanted and end his life for him.

'Frank and me are gunna have some fun with your pretty daughter whether you like it or not, old man,' the fellow said in a no-nonsense manner. 'We ain't had a woman in a long time, an' so I reckon it's high time we did.'

'You just ride on out of here an' keep on ridin',' Jeff shouted, only with a heap less confidence being displayed in his voice this time.

'You're starting to annoy me, old-timer,' the man said. 'A woman like that little gal was made for fun, and Frank an' me aim to have our fill of her, an' we ain't gunna let you stand in our way.' He started to dismount.

'Step down from that horse and you're a dead man!' Zach said in a loud and authoritative tone.

The man froze for a second before swinging his back-side back where it had been.

'You two barrel-boarders are trespassing. I suggest you turn your horses around and get your mangy carcases off this ranch.'

The one named Frank looked Zach up and down as he stood there facing the two horseman. 'It's seems to me this must be the little gal's sweetheart, Lem,' he said to the other man, without taking his eyes off Zach for a second.

'Yep, I reckon you'd be right 'bout that, Frank.'

'Do you reckon we should do as he says and ride on out of here, Frank?' the question was asked with the greatest of levity.

'Yep, I reckon we should, Lem,' his friend said, answering him in the same vein. 'And we'll do it too, right after we've each taken a turn with his woman.'

Both men laughed.

Zachariah Thompson stood his ground, his dark eyes watching and waiting. He knew this wasn't going to end without bloodshed. But what remained to be seen was whose blood it would be.

'I'm not going to tell you again.' Zach stood fifteen feet or so away, his right hand resting against the cool leather of his holster, his palm ready to close around the wooden grips of the .44, and his index finger primed to find the trigger.

'There's two of us and only one of you,' Frank reminded him. 'You ain't in any position to be giving us any orders.'

'That's what you think.'

Frank looked the stranger up and down. He didn't look much standing there in his tattered clothes, but those dark eyes spoke of something sinister, something he couldn't quite put his finger on, but which he knew spelled trouble.

'Come on, Frank,' Lem said, unable to disguise his boredom, 'let's get on with this. I'm sick of all this talk. I want some action with the little woman.'

Frank's sixth sense was kicking in. His gut was telling him that the stranger was a force to be reckoned with. But he and Lem had made their intentions known, and now he felt they were committed to seeing things through. Without any warning he suddenly made a grab for the Remington on his hip.

Zach's gun hand swept up with a gracefulness that was only surpassed in impressiveness by the speed with which the .44 left its holster. The burst of flame that spat from the old Colt's barrel immediately gave way to a stream of smoke as Frank's chest took the full brunt of the impact from the lump of lead that slammed into him. Lurching back in the saddle, his Remington dropped from his hand and fell, coming to rest on the ground at his mare's feet.

The .44 was immediately pointed in Lem's direction, and although the saddle tramp managed to clear leather he never got to fire off a shot. Another bullet from Zach's six-gun roared on its way, punching a hole in Lem in pretty much the same spot on his body that Frank had copped it. Both men dropped from their saddles no more than a few seconds apart.

'Dang, that's gotta be about the fastest I've ever seen a man pull iron in my entire life,' Jeff gushed excitedly, as he stared down at the two men who were taking in their final breaths.

The whole thing had played itself out so quick that Zach hadn't had a chance to think about it. One moment he was warning the men off, and the next his .44 had been in his hand spitting death. He had no idea how he had pulled it off – it was as if the gun had been in his hand all the time.

'I reckon maybe Zachariah Thompson's a whole heap more'n he's been lettin' on, Emily,' Jeff said to his daughter. 'No ordinary man can handle a gun like he just has.'

'I … I didn't know that I could handle a gun like that,' Zach said, his head full of confusion over what had just happened.

'Well, that hand of yours sure knew what to do,' Jeff pointed out. 'An' thank the Lord for Emmy an' me that it did, 'cos there ain't no prizes for guessin' what would've happened to the pair of us if you hadn't dealt with 'em.'

Emily hadn't said a word the entire time. Her eyes were riveted on the dead men, and the sight of their blood rapidly spilling out and beginning to pool on the ground around them. It was then that Zach realized she had never seen somebody die before.

'Are you all right, Emily?' he asked, as he slipped the Colt back in its holster, and stepping closer to her, he placed his hand on her shoulder.

She shuddered involuntarily, and then giving a little cry, turned and ran back into the house.

'She'll be all right, lad,' Jeff assured him. 'She's just been through a terrible ordeal, but she's a tough lass an' she'll come right.'

Zach had to admit that he was feeling a little shaky himself. He didn't know whether he had ever killed a man before, but he couldn't say that he felt good about the fact he had just laid these two fellows in the dust, despite the fact they had been planning to commit a heinous crime. This business of not knowing anything about his past was starting to trouble him. How had he been able to handle that old .44 the way he had? Just who was he?

'We'd best get rid of these bodies,' Jeff said, breaking Zach free of his musings. 'I'll get the horses hitched up to the buckboard so we can cart 'em away. Might pay if we bury 'em somewhere out on the ranch where no one'll find 'em.'

Zach nodded. As Jeff moved off to see to the task he turned and headed for the house.

'I'm sorry you had to witness that,' Zach said to Emily when he had found her in the kitchen. She had her back up against the wall as if she were hiding from something, and the tears were streaming down her face.

'You and Pa could have been killed by those two men,' she said shakily. 'And if you hadn't been here,' a sob escaped her. 'If you hadn't been here ... then I ...' she broke down then, and so he crossed the floor and took her gently in his arms.

'It's all over now,' he said softly. 'It was horrible, but you can't let this get to you.'

She snuggled in close, the warmth and voluptuousness of her body sending waves of pure pleasure coursing through him. She was woman enough to cause him to lose control of his faculties if he wasn't careful, and what frightened him was that he was definitely losing the desire to remain careful.

'I'm glad you are here, Zach,' she said when she had brought her tears under control. 'Pa couldn't have stood up to those two men. Not even if he had been wearing his gun. They would have killed him before he could even have drawn on them.'

He didn't say anything, just continued to hold her in his arms as if she had always belonged to him.

'I will be sad when you move on.' She looked up into his face then. 'And what will we do if men like that come back again and you aren't here to protect us?'

He couldn't answer that. What would they do? Emily would always be too much of a temptation for men like Frank and Lem, men who allowed their baser instincts to rule their actions. It got him to thinking about how Jeff had managed to survive here for so long on his own. Surely Frank and Lem weren't the first drifters to have stumbled across the Fawcett ranch house. It made Zach sick to his stomach to think what could and probably would happen to Emily one day in the future. Jeff really had no call keeping her here, knowing the likelihood of something terrible happening to her was so high. She was a refined woman, and as such belonged in polite society – somewhere she could shine and show the world how special she really was.

He gently broke the embrace. She really was getting to him. He was loco to be thinking like this. It wouldn't be long before he was thinking about marrying her and settling down if he didn't get a grip on himself. 'I'll help your pa bury those fellers now,' he said, then without uttering another word turned and made his way outside to help Jeff with the unpleasant task.

****

Zach looked up from the bottom of the hole. His clothes were wringing wet with sweat, and almost every muscle in his body was aching. 'Just how deep does this grave have to be?' he asked, hoping that Jeff would tell him he had dug far enough already.

'Another foot or so I reckon. We don't want the wild critters diggin' 'em up do we?'

'I suppose not,' Zach conceded, although right about now he didn't much care what happened to the corpses, he was so dog tired.

Half an hour later Zach handed his shovel to Jeff and climbed on out after it. 'That's some hard ground you've got there, Jeff,' he said, as he dusted his trousers down.

'Yep, it can make a man break out in a sweat just lookin' at it.'

It had certainly made Zach break out in a sweat, although he couldn't say the same for the older man. He had merely watched proceedings from ground level, and Zach doubted being a spectator had caused him to perspire at all.

'Give me a hand tossin' these two barrel-boarders in,' Jeff said as he grabbed Frank by the wrists.

Zach picked up the dead man's ankles and helped drag the corpse off the buckboard, and then between the two of them they carried it over to the edge of the hole.

'No need to stand on ceremony,' Jeff said as he swung Frank out over the hastily dug grave and let go.

Zach released his hold a split second later and then watched as the body thumped heavily on to the stony bed it was destined to occupy for the rest of eternity.

'One more, an' then we can cover 'em over an' head for home,' Jeff said, almost gleefully Zach felt.

Twenty minutes later, after they had levelled the top of the grave, and then rolled several large rocks on top so no wild animal would disturb the surface, alerting a passerby to the fact that someone was buried there, Zach dumped his shovel on the back of the buckboard and gratefully climbed up on the seat beside Jeff. He couldn't remember, but he doubted he had worked this hard in years. At least, that was what his body was trying to tell him right now.

Jeff Fawcett gave a quick flick of the reins and the buckboard rumbled off over the uneven ground, the mare pulling it keen to get back to the barn so she could enjoy its shade and take in a draft of cool water.

'You know what, Zach? I reckon you shouldn't be in such an all-fired hurry to head off now that you're on the mend.'

Zach glanced at his companion for a moment. 'Why's that?'

'I've been doin' me some thinkin'. You really ain't got no idea why you're in this part of the country, have you?'

'No, Jeff, I haven't.'

'So then there's no real reason for you to be hurryin' along?'

'No, I guess there isn't.' He was wondering where this was all heading.

'I sure could do with some help around here. I couldn't pay much mind, but then you ain't got nothin' lined up neither, so I reckon it'd profit us both if you stayed on here a while.'

Zach had to admit that the suggestion did make sense. He hadn't had any idea what to do with himself, seeing as he really didn't know anything about himself except his name. So there wasn't any employment lined up for him anywhere, and if he left the Fawcetts behind he would be merely riding off into the unknown, and that didn't appeal to him at all.

'All right, Jeff,' he said eventually, 'I'll take you up on your offer. For a while at least anyway, just until I get my memory back.'

'Well now, that's just fine.' He shot a glance at the young man seated beside him. 'I think Emmy will be pleased to have you around, too.'

Zach kept his eyes on the trail ahead and said nothing. So that was the old man's game. He was match making. He was getting on in years and must be worrying about what was going to happen to his daughter after he was gone. Then, of course, given the way Zach had handled the situation with Frank and Lem earlier on, the old fellow must be thinking that he had found the right man to look after his little girl, a man who could stand up to trouble when it presented itself and acquit himself well. It placed Zach in a difficult situation, and as lovely as Emily was, he wasn't sure he wanted to settle down with her for the rest of his life on a barren piece of dirt he would have to work himself into the ground trying to scrape a living off it.

As they headed back the mile or so to the house, Zach thought his situation over. He really didn't have anywhere to go while he was still unsure of who he was. The name Zachariah Thompson wasn't much to go on. He wasn't even sure of what line of work he was in. Looking down at the blistered hands, rubbed raw courtesy of the shovel handle, he knew it wasn't something physical or they wouldn't be in the state they were right now. He didn't think he knew too much about cows, or putting up fences, or any of the other jobs that required doing on a ranch – but at least he would have his food and board, and maybe a little money until he could figure out where his future lay.

FOUR

Zach looked back along the line of posts he had painstakingly dug in, and felt a surge of pride. He had laboured for days to erect this fence, and it was certainly beginning to look impressive, even if he did say so himself. This manual labour lark might be hard work, but the satisfaction he derived from the end result was worth every single muscle-aching second of it. Whenever Jeff rode out to check on his progress, Zach found himself holding his head high, especially seeing the old man was so complimentary about Zach's efforts, and it had Zach wondering if owning a ranch of his own one day mightn't be such a bad idea.

The stunningly clear skies and surroundings spoke volumes to Zach as well. He could get lost in the beauty of the landscape. What he had only days before seen as a barren landscape had now come alive to him, and so he had developed a new appreciation for what his Creator had fashioned.

'That's as good a fence as I could ever have put up,' Jeff conceded, when he had ridden up to see how Zach was doing later that afternoon. He chuckled, 'Actually, as much as I hate to admit it, it's better'n I could put up.'

'Thanks, Jeff, your praise means a lot to me, especially seeing as it comes from you.'

'With an extra man here we'll get through a whole heap more'n I ever could alone. That'll make the ranch easier to manage.' He gazed along the length of erected fence and smiled. 'This'll stop the beeves from wanderin' off out there in the badlands an' windin' up crow bait or in the hands of the Apache. That on its own will make the ranch more profitable.'

It made sense, even Zach could see that. The fewer cattle that were either lost or stolen, meant the more cattle there would be to collect money on come selling time. The more head the ranch could carry through to maturity meant more cash coming the way of the Fawcetts, making Emily's life so much easier than it otherwise would be, and that was something that had become dear to Zach's heart these past few weeks.

'I kinda get the impression you've enjoyed yourself lately,' Jeff said at the end of the working day, as they rode on back to the house later that afternoon. He had made the comment tentatively, as if he was unsure whether he should proceed with what he was going to say next.

Zach just nodded, eager to hear what the older man had to say.

'In that case I reckon the time has come to offer you a permanent job here.' He cast a sideways glance at Zach as they rode along side by side. 'You've got my permission to court Emily as well.'

Zach swallowed down the lump that had formed in his throat. Had he just heard right? Had Jeff Fawcett just said Zach could make a play for his daughter?

'I figure you like her. I've seen the way you look at her, an' it's easy to see she's well an' truly smitten with you. I've got no son to leave the place to when I'm gone, so the place'd be yours I reckon, if you were to marry her.'

'It sounds like you've been giving this a whole heap of thought.'

'Haven't thought about much else these past few days,' Jeff confessed. 'Emmy means a lot to me, an' so I want to see her well taken care of before I shuffle off.'

'You ain't ailing none are you?' Zach asked quickly.

'No, nothin' like that, lad. I would just like to see her settled in case somethin' unexpected happens to me, an' if'n that does happen, then I reckon you'd be the right man to take care of her.'

Zach had harboured his suspicions for a while now that the old man had been thinking along these lines. He had dropped little hints here and there, no doubt to sound Zach out before he came right out with it. But it still came as a shock to Zach to actually hear the fellow voice the whole idea and wait on an answer to it.

'I like Emily just fine, Jeff, and I think you know that.'

'But …?'

'Dang it, Jeff, I don't even know who I am, let alone what I should be doing. None of my past has come back to

33

me yet, and it's beginning to look like it never will. I'm not up to making plans like getting wed and settling down. Not yet, at any road.'

'Maybe I'm pushin' you a little too soon. I don't want to railroad you into doin' somethin' you might regret later on. Just think on it for a while, an' when you're ready, let me know what you've decided.'

'That's fair enough, I reckon. I'm not ready to move on yet, anyhow.'

'Take as long as you need … just as long as you need,' Jeff urged. The longer Zach Thompson stuck around, the surer Jeff was that he would never leave. Emily would work her magic on him, and then the young man would reach the point where leaving would be the last thing on his mind. Yep, Jeff liked the idea of having young Zach Thompson for a son-in-law. He was good with a gun, which meant Emily would be in safe hands if any more unsavoury characters were to come calling unexpectedly, and he wasn't afraid to roll up his sleeves and put in a hard day's work. He could think of a whole lot worse fellers who could be wedded to his beloved daughter, but he couldn't think of one single better one. As far as he was concerned the whole thing was settled – all that remained was for young Zach Thompson to agree to it.

Zach was sitting on the bottom step of the porch that evening after supper was over when Emily slipped outside to join him. He had just lit up a cheroot and was staring up at the stars with the kind of wonder usually reserved for small children, when she sat down beside him.

'I hope you don't mind me smoking,' he said, as she settled herself comfortably on the step.

'I know most women complain about the smell, Zach, but I have to confess I rather like it.'

He smiled at her. 'Would you like to try it?'

She stared at him for a moment, 'What ... you mean *me* smoke?'

'Why not ... why should I be the one to have all the fun?'

She glanced nervously over her shoulder as if she was worried someone may have heard.

'I won't tell your pa if you don't.' He held the cheroot out to her.

'What do I do?' she asked, as she took it from him.

'Just suck on it, and then let the smoke roll back down your throat a little way before blowing it back out.'

She did as he had suggested, and grinned at him when the grey smoke streamed out from between her lips.

'You did well. Most men cough their lungs out the first time they try it.'

'I've seen some men blow smoke out their nostrils. How do they do that?'

'Draw the smoke in like you did the first time, only when you exhale, keep your lips tightly closed and the smoke'll come out your nose.'

Emily tried it. The pungent smell of burnt tobacco tickled her nostrils as it worked its way out, but she experienced a feeling of euphoria as two streams of smoke jetted away from her face to mingle with the cool night air.

'No one would guess you hadn't been smoking for years.'

She giggled, and the sound of her sweet voice engaged in mirth filled him with delight. He found himself living for the evenings when she would join him out here on the porch and chat for a while. He was even starting to think of her when he was out on the ranch working. Yes, he was falling for her, there was no doubt in his mind about that. If he didn't leave the ranch very soon he would be in over his head, and the problem was, he wasn't sure whether that was what he wanted or not.

She handed the cigar back to him. 'I enjoyed that, but I can't see myself making a habit of it. Maybe I can just have a puff on yours now and again.'

He grinned at her. 'I think that can be arranged.'

'Zach ... have you given any thought to staying on here permanently?'

'I've given it plenty of thought, Emily, but it's too early to say what I'll do yet. I'm really hoping I'll get my memory back soon. You see, I might even have a wife somewhere that I don't know about.' He saw the fear come into her eyes and realized she hadn't for one moment considered he may be married. But it was a possibility. It was a very real possibility indeed.

'I ... I ... hope that you aren't,' she said, rushing the last part out so quickly that she had to take a sudden breath to steady herself.

He looked into her eyes and smiled gently at her. 'So do I, Emily.'

'So you are leaning towards staying then?'

'I never said that. I still need time. You must give me that time without putting pressure on me to stay.'

She looked downcast. 'It's just that ... I ... oh, Zach!' she suddenly got up and with a sob rushed back into the house so he wouldn't see the tears that had flooded her eyes.

Zach couldn't claim to understand women, but he was fairly certain her emotional outburst was due to her fear he was going to leave and she would never see him again, and that event was certainly a distinct possibility. He couldn't say he would be happy if it did come down to leaving her behind and never seeing her again, but he was realistic enough to accept that that was what it might come down to in the end.

Flicking the stub of his cheroot into the shrubbery in front of the porch, Zach stood up and wandered over to the corral; he rested his arms on the top rail and gazed absentmindedly up at those stars again. This dang memory loss was putting his life on hold. He couldn't make the decision to stay and take up with Emily, and he couldn't make the decision to leave, not without knowing exactly who he was, and whether or not he had a woman, and maybe even kids somewhere.

He owed so much to Jeff Fawcett, and his daughter, come to that. Yep, he owed them his very life, and so he hated the thought that he might have to run out on them one day soon. If he suddenly got his memory back, then his departure might have to be just as sudden. There might be barely enough time to say goodbye. If only his wretched memory would return and let him know who he was and where he came from, because the not knowing was slowly torturing him.

A meteorite flashed across the dark sky, its fiery arc putting on a brilliant display for a few seconds before fizzling out almost as quickly as it had appeared. He figured a man's life was pretty much the same as that shooting star. He came from nowhere, burned brightly for a short time, and then disappeared without a trace. His time on earth was so short, and if he botched it up then his life would have been all for nothing. Zach had no desire to waste the years he had left. He might not ever find out exactly who he really was, besides knowing his name was Zachariah Thompson, but he was determined he wasn't going to amount to nothing. He had come close to death twice in the past few weeks, and that had given him an appreciation of life, an appreciation that would drive him to make every second of every minute of every hour a celebration of that life.

FIVE

They had swept upon the small herd of horses so swiftly and so silently that Zach hadn't even heard them coming, but there they were, expertly driving off the herd right before his very eyes. Dropping the hammer he had been using to staple the barbed wire to the fence posts, he made a mad dash for the buckboard to retrieve the rifle, calling to Jeff to attract his attention to the danger as he did so.

There were eight Apache in all, and they didn't seem to be having any trouble moving away the twenty-five horses that belonged to the Fawcett ranch at a fair pace. Sliding the Winchester off the deck of the buckboard, Zach levered a round through and took aim. He didn't like killing a man in this fashion, but they really had no right to take what didn't belong to them.

His first shot went wide of the mark, and he silently chided himself for having rushed it. Making a concerted effort to control his nerves, he fed another round through, and taking aim squeezed the trigger.

A young warrior lurched forward on his pony, a crimson patch blossoming on his right shoulder. He shouted something to one of his comrades, who spun his mount around and, letting out a war whoop, charged at Zach.

'Of all the dang fool things to do,' Zach muttered, as he levered the next round through and, resting the Winchester on the side of the buckboard, took careful aim.

But just as he fired the Apache slipped off the pony's back to cling to the animal's side, so he was invisible to Zach.

'You cunning son-of-a-gun!' Zach figured he knew what the Apache's game was. He would pop up and fire at Zach just as he reached the buckboard, and so grappling with the lever of the Winchester again he made sure another shell slipped into the firing mechanism.

The young warrior had urged his pony to go faster, so fast that Zach hadn't given himself time to react, so he was caught totally off guard when the animal launched itself into the air, its front legs tucked up near its belly, as it sailed gracefully over the buckboard to land somewhere behind him.

Despite the suddenness of it all, Zach Thompson still had the presence of mind to dive to the ground, narrowly missing the bullet fired from the Apache's rifle even before the pony's hoofs touched the ground. Rolling over he immediately took aim and fired, trusting to his luck that he would hit something. He wasn't to be disappointed. The Apache dropped from the pony's back and hit the hard ground, rolling over twice before lying motionless.

Unwilling to take a chance, Zach fired again, the lead from his rifle thumping into the torso of the man and making absolutely sure he would never present a threat again.

Jeff arrived at that moment with his Henry rifle in his hand and completely out of breath. Without saying a word to Zach he crawled under the buckboard and commenced a steady stream of fire. Two more Apache met their deaths at the hands of the two white men – but despite their losses the raiding party still managed to sequester the horses.

'Dang it, I can't afford to lose 'em,' Jeff complained, as the horses and the Apache who had driven them off disappeared over a rise and therefore at a safe distance from rifle fire. 'It's bad enough they've taken some of the beef, but without those horses to sell to the army I don't know how I'll make ends meet.'

'Do you want to saddle up and go after them?'

Jeff gave it some thought. 'No, I don't think it'd be wise,' he said eventually. 'I figure there's more of 'em out there just waitin' for us to try somethin' like that. It ain't worth losin' our lives over. There'd be no one to look after Emmy then, an' if they came back as far as the house an' found her alone there's no tellin' what they'd do to her.'

Zach had a fairly good idea. He had heard that the Apache often took white women captive, and they weren't always treated well. He was determined he wasn't going to let that happen to Emily. So Jeff was right, it was best just to suffer the loss and live to fight another day.

'Maybe we'd best head home just in case they come back,' Zach suggested. 'We can defend ourselves much better from there. Out here we'd be at their mercy if they came at us in any great number, and they'll be back, if only to collect their dead.'

'I reckon you're right, lad. Let's hook the mare to the buckboard and hightail it out of here.'

That night as Zach smoked his cheroot out on the porch he gave some serious thought to the past week's events. What with white men turning up at the ranch house with evil intent on their minds, and now Apache bands roving the ranch stealing horses and cattle and not afraid to exchange gunfire, the idea of settling down here permanently was rapidly beginning to lose its appeal for Zach. A man couldn't make something of his life if he were dead, and death was a very real possibility if he stayed on here. He couldn't understand how Jeff could place his daughter in such danger, knowing it must only be a matter of time before something terrible happened to one or both of them. If Zach hadn't been here when Frank and Lem had drifted in, then that moment would have arrived already. Nope, Zach was beginning to think that Jeff Fawcett was a selfish old man clinging to this barren piece of dirt for no other reason than his foolish pride.

It wasn't as if the ranch brought in a good living, either – in which case staying on as long as Jeff had might have been justified. But the Fawcetts were merely scratching out their existence, and so there was really no excuse for placing Emily in such danger. The more he thought about it, the angrier Zach began to feel. Maybe with the horses gone, and the Apache constantly stealing a few head of cattle at regular intervals, Jeff might be persuaded to sell up and try his hand at something more profitable, somewhere far safer than here.

Getting up from the chair he had been sitting on, Zach stepped off the porch and headed over to the well to get himself a drink. The bucket was already raised, so he lifted the tin cup off the nail it was hanging from, dipped it into the bucket and brought the sweet-tasting water to his lips. Having slaked his thirst, he had just hung the cup back up when the sound of a horse whinnying drifted to him on the night air.

What was odd was that it hadn't come from the corral where the only horses the ranch had left were contained. A shot of fear raced through him as it suddenly dawned on him that it must be the Apache, who had returned to avenge the death of their comrades. No sooner had he had this thought than an arrow thumped into the post beside his head, just missing the tin cup where it dangled from the nail. They were obviously intent on taking him out silently, so those in the house wouldn't be alerted to the fact that an attack was imminent. Turning on his heel, he sprinted back to the house to raise the alarm.

'Jeff … Jeff …' he hollered as he raced across the porch to the front door, barrelling through without any thought for the safety of anyone who might be unfortunate enough to be standing too close on the other side. 'Jeff … the Apache are here!'

Jeff Fawcett sprang from his armchair as if he were a man in his twenties, and wrenching open the cabinet that held the ranch's store of rifles, turned his face to the open door of the room. 'Emily,' he roared at the top of his lungs, 'get downstairs right away!'

Zach burst into the room, his heart beating wildly in his chest.

'How many are there?' Jeff asked as he hurriedly began to load his Henry rifle.

'Don't know. I didn't hang around to count them.' He grabbed the Winchester Jeff held out to him, and reached into the cabinet to pull out a box of shells.

'Dang it, where is that girl?' Jeff exclaimed. 'Emily!' he shouted again, 'get yourself down here immediately!'

'There's no need to scream your head off, Pa,' she said as she bustled into the room to see what all the fuss was about, 'I heard you the first time. Now, what's this all about?'

'The Apache are outside,' he said bluntly, without taking his eyes off the task of loading his rifle.

Zach glanced at Emily long enough to see that her face had gone as white as a sheet. 'It'll be all right,' he said in a vain attempt to calm her fears. But he knew they were up against it this time. This wasn't going to be some little skirmish. The Apache were here for retribution, and he knew they wouldn't stop until they had satisfied their blood lust.

'Turn out the lights in the house, an' then start loadin' the spare rifles for Zach an' me,' Jeff ordered. 'Just keep the one lamp burnin', but turn it down low. Just enough light so you can see what you're doin'. Do you understand?'

Despite the fear that threatened to possess her, Emily nodded.

'Then off you go, girl, quick as you can. The sooner we douse the lights in the house the better.'

Zach moved over to a window facing the front yard, and opening it, peered out into the darkness. Thankfully the light of a half moon made it possible to pick up any movement that wasn't too far off.

'They've never done this before,' Jeff said as he took up his position at a window on the other side of the room. 'They've only ever stolen horses an' cattle. They haven't attacked the house.'

'Have you ever killed any of them before?'

'Nope, I don't reckon I have. Fired at 'em now an' again when they tried to run my stock off, but I doubt I ever hit one of 'em.'

'Well, we sure did hit some of them earlier on today,' Zach said dryly, 'and now they're here to even the score.' He didn't know how many of them were out there, but if they had turned up in any great number then things could end very badly for the Fawcett household, they could end very badly indeed.

Zach fancied he could see something streaking across the yard towards the barn and so flicking the Winchester to eye level lined it up and fired.

'Get anythin'?' Jeff asked eagerly from across the room where he was straining to make out any movement in the darkness outside.

'Someone went to ground but I don't know whether that's because I hit him or he's just playing dead.'

'Put another bullet in him to make sure.'

Taking his time over his shot this time, Zach punched out another round and saw the body take the hit.

'Any good?'

'Well, I got him, and he's not getting up, so I reckon that's him taken care of.'

'I wish I knew how many of 'em are skulkin' around out there.' He tore his eyes away from the window. 'Where's that girl,' he said irritably, 'we're gunna need her help any minute now.'

'Don't panic, Pa, I'm right here,' Emily said as she swept into the room.

'Well get yourself loadin' them rifles up just as fast as you can. Zach an' me are gunna be too busy to do it ourselves when they make their move.'

Zach thought Emily seemed surprisingly unruffled, given the fact that at any moment a bunch of bloodthirsty Apache could burst through the door looking to lift their scalps. Her initial shock at being told they were about to be under attack had given way to a calm resolve to help out in any way she could.

An arrow suddenly whished through the window and struck the sofa, its flaming shaft igniting the fabric almost immediately.

'Quickly, Emily,' Jeff bawled, 'put it out!'

Dropping the rifle she was in the process of loading, Emily Fawcett snatched up the rug off her father's armchair and did her best to smother the flames with it. Thanks to her quick action she soon had the flames out before they had a chance to really take hold.

Jeff starting firing rapidly, the bullets spitting from the Henry in quick succession as he tried to stop whoever it was that was trying to rush the house. 'Got him!' he said triumphantly, as an Apache warrior nose-dived into the dirt.

The sound of the back door being forced open reached Zach's ears, so he abandoned the window and raced across the room and into the hallway, just as the oak door gave way and three men spilled inside. He had time to fire once … twice … and then the third man was upon him, so they both crashed to the floor, struggling over the scalping knife the young Apache was trying to plunge into Zach.

Back in the room, Jeff's Henry was working overtime. It wasn't just a small party of braves they were up against, it was obviously a large raiding party.

The Apache grappling with Zach was on top now, trying his best to position his weight over the knife he gripped tightly in both hands so he could force it downwards, Zach's unprotected chest being the target.

Zach couldn't believe the strength of the fellow. He was young and fit, a perfect specimen of manhood, and right now he was having the best of the contest. If Zach didn't turn this around, and turn it around fast, then it was going to be over in double quick time.

He could hear more warriors enter through the shattered door, but he had his hands full just trying to keep that knife away from his heart, so could do nothing about it. Then he heard a swishing of skirts and suddenly Emily was there, a shotgun in her hands, and without a moment's

47

hesitation she discharged both barrels at the unwelcome visitors.

The double boom of the shotgun going off close to his ears distracted Zach's assailant just long enough for Zach to turn the tables on him. Flipping him over, he twisted the man's wrists down and lent his entire weight to the effort of driving the blade into the warrior's chest, a sudden gasp of surprise being the only sound the defeated man made before he closed his eyes and passed to the next life.

Leaping to his feet Zach reached for his .44, and fired twice at the tumble of bodies that were spilling through the door. Emily in the meantime had replaced the spent cartridges, and the shotgun roared in her hands once more, wreaking death and destruction amongst the Apache who had been foolish enough to try and gain entry to the house.

Zach worked feverishly to pull the dead bodies away from the door so he could close it, and succeeded in doing so before any more of the Apache appeared. 'Help me drag the Hutch dresser over to the door,' he shouted to Emily as he grappled with the heavy piece of furniture. The pair of them managed to slide it across to barricade the door, then Zach piled the half dozen bodies in front of it to make sure it couldn't be pushed out of the way in a hurry. But although this barricade might keep the Apache from getting into the house through this particular door again, Zach knew it would only be a matter of time before they found another way in.

'I need to go help Pa reload,' Emily said, before disappearing back into the room her father was defending. Seconds later her ear-shattering scream reached Zach's ears, so abandoning his plans to barricade the door at the other end of the hallway, he raced into the room to see what the matter was.

Jeff Fawcett lay flat on his back, a neat hole punched in his forehead, the result of an Apache bullet. Jeff must have exposed his face for a moment too long at the window, and that was all it had taken for the death-dealing shot to strike home.

'Pa ... Pa,' Emily wailed, all thoughts of staving off the attack gone from her mind due to the intense grief that overwhelmed her.

Zach could smell smoke. Risking a quick peek out of the same window that had cost Jeff his life, he was alarmed to see the side of the house on fire: hungry flames were gnawing at the dry timbers with an alacrity that told him the entire house would soon be swallowed up in a gigantic inferno. The Apache must have cut brush and stacked it against the wall of the house, then set it alight. The situation was critical – if they remained for much longer then they would certainly die.

The Apache had retreated to a safe distance to watch and wait, no doubt satisfied that the flames would deal with the white men inside the house and save them from losing any more warriors. But Zach knew that as soon as he and Emily stepped outside they would be met by a hail of bullets. It was a classic case of damned if they did, and damned if they didn't.

As Emily knelt on the wooden floor and cradled her dead father in her arms, Zach's mind raced. How was he going to get them out of this? Within ten minutes the whole place was going to be ablaze. In fact, the smoke would probably kill them long before the flames did, and so they had considerably less than ten minutes to find a way out if they wanted to live.

An idea suddenly came to him. 'Emily, does the house have a cellar?'

She looked up at him through tearstained eyes. 'Yes, the door to the cellar is under the stairs.'

He quickly thought things over. The cellar would only be any good until the fire robbed it of oxygen or the burning timbers collapsed into it. Either way they would eventually die ... unless?

'Is there any way leading out of the cellar?'

'Pa dug a shaft that comes up several yards away from the house so he could drop cut firewood down into the cellar. It comes up right beside the woodshed.'

'Is it big enough for a man to get through?'

'I don't know, Zach. But he would tip a wheelbarrow load of firewood down it each time.'

That sounded like it might be large enough to take a human body. They had no other choice, anyway. They couldn't rush outside, and they couldn't stay where they were. The cellar and that shaft was their only hope.

The noise the flames were making was almost deafening now, and Zach found himself shouting to be heard. 'We have to head for the cellar right now, Emily.'

'I can't leave Pa.'

'He's dead, Emily. There's nothing more we can do for him.'

'We can give him a decent burial.'

'We can't get him outside without those Apache killing us,' he pointed out.

'We can take him down into the cellar with us.'

He could see he was going to have trouble getting her to move unless he agreed to the crazy idea, so he nodded, then bent down and hauled the tall man upright, and slung him across his shoulder and headed for the door. 'Grab that lamp you were using and then open the cellar door for me, Emily,' he shouted.

Brushing past him, Emily reached the cellar door before he did and had it open before he arrived. She slowly negotiated the rough wooden steps, illuminating the way for Zach as she descended.

Zach could hear the inferno over his head as the flames reached the main body of the house. They hadn't left the death-trap upstairs a moment too soon. Reaching the bottom of the stairs he laid Jeff gently on the dirt floor of the cellar. 'Show me this shaft,' he said as calmly as he could, hoping that it would prove to be their salvation, but fearing that it wouldn't be. Already there was smoke seeping under the door at the top of the stairs, and he knew it wouldn't be long before the heat from above began to cook them and they would be gasping for air.

Emily led him over to where there was a narrow opening in the rammed earth wall of the cellar with a shaft that slanted up towards the yard outside. 'Dang it, that's gunna be tight,' he mumbled to himself as he held the lamp at the opening and peered along the length of the shaft.

The temperature had just gone up a few degrees. He could feel the cool air of the cellar beginning to disappear. Soon it would be uncomfortably hot, and not long after that oppressive. They would die if they didn't use this shaft very soon.

'Come here, Emily,' he called softly to the young woman who had returned to cradling her father's lifeless head in her lap.

She gently laid his head down on the floor of the cellar and went to him.

'I'm going to crouch down and I want you to stand on my shoulders; when I stand up, you will be partway up the shaft. Then I'll place my palms on the heels of your shoes and push you as far up as I can. You'll have to scramble the rest of the way out on your own.'

She looked back at her father. 'How are you going to get Pa out?'

'We are going to have to leave him here, Emily.'

A sob escaped her. 'I'm not going without Pa.'

The temperature had risen yet again, and Zach's nostrils were telling him the air was getting stuffier by the second. The fire above their heads was drawing the oxygen under the cellar door to feed its insatiable appetite. Time really wasn't on their side.

'There's no way we can get him through that shaft,' Zach pointed out as gently as he could. 'And even if we could, we don't have the time to do it. If we don't move right now we'll both be dead within the next five minutes or so.'

Another sob burst forth. 'I wanted to give him a decent burial.'

'I know you did. But I'm sure Jeff would want you to live rather than die trying to give him that burial.'

Even in her distressed state she could see the wisdom in what he said. 'All right, I'll do what you say.'

Bending over he let her climb on to his back, then she placed her feet on his shoulders, steadying herself with her hands by placing them against the wall of the cellar.

He offered up a silent prayer of thanks that she was so petite. If she had been a hefty girl then things might have been very different. 'Are you ready?'

'Yes,' she said simply, her eyes on the wooden cover at the end of the shaft, hoping all the while that she would be able to lift it so she could climb out.

'Here we go then.' He straightened up, and her head and torso disappeared into the shaft. Waiting just long enough to steady himself he grasped her ankles and used all his strength to force her body as far along as he could. 'You're on your own now.'

He felt her feet leave his hands as she managed to get a foothold on the crumbling dirt sides of the shaft. 'When you get out, lie flat on your stomach and wait there for me,' he ordered. 'Whatever you do don't move or they'll spot you.'

He could barely breathe now. The air had dwindled to such an extent he was beginning to feel dozy. He must get out of the cellar immediately or he was going to end up spending all eternity there with Jeff.

A sudden rush of cool, fresh air rushed down the shaft to hit him in the face. Emily must have lifted the wooden cover and made it outside. With a sigh of relief he used what little strength he had left to haul himself up into the shaft, all the while hoping he wouldn't be too big to squeeze his way through to safety.

He struggled to get his boots to hold on the crumbling dirt. Being much heavier and larger than Emily the damage he was doing to the walls of the shaft was hindering his progress. His boots were merely slipping against the disintegrating dirt rather than making a solid purchase that would enable him to force his way upwards.

A loud crash echoed in the cellar below, and a sudden blast of heat slammed into his legs. The floor above the cellar had collapsed, and Jeff now had his burial, albeit not the one that his daughter had in mind – and if Zach didn't hurry up the shaft was going to cave in, sending Zach down there to join him.

With a supreme effort he grappled his way through the narrow opening until he felt his hands make contact with the ground outside, then heaving himself upwards, came to rest beside Emily, his lungs near bursting from the effort and for want of fresh air.

With the chopping block and the mound of cut firewood that Jeff hadn't got around to dumping down the shaft to shield them from sight, he lay flat on his stomach and turned his head to look at the house – and was instantly stunned by what he saw. The place was all but gone – the roof and two sides had toppled in, and the flames were leaping high into the night sky. There was no way they would have survived if they had been foolish enough to have stayed and fought the blaze.

He figured the Apache would have left by now. They would have assumed that because the occupants of the house hadn't come rushing out, they had perished in the inferno. After taking the horses from the corral and whatever they found of use in the barn, they would have left, satisfied that they had avenged the death of their people.

'Can I move now?' Emily whispered, 'the fire is scorching me.'

'Just give me a chance to look around.' Crawling to the edge of the woodpile Zach turned his head in the direction of the barn, his eyes using the light cast by the conflagration to see if anyone remained. The horses in the corral were gone, and the barn door was open, but he couldn't see any movement anywhere that led him to believe the Apache were still here. 'Let's just lie here very still for another fifteen minutes or so to make absolutely sure,' he said. 'I know the heat from the fire is hard to take, but it won't kill us. However, if the Apache are still here they definitely will.'

SIX

Zach got slowly to his knees and cautiously looked around. The house had completely collapsed now, and would burn on for another hour or so until the flames had consumed all that was left to consume. The Apache were definitely gone, and he doubted they would be back. As far as they were concerned all the white people on this ranch were now dead, and anything of value had been taken.

'You can get up now, Emily,' he said quietly.

Emily Fawcett gradually got to her feet, not wanting to see the destruction of the house that had been her home all her life, nor dwell on the fact that her beloved father was lying beneath all that smouldering timber and ash.

Zach made a sudden grab for her as her legs gave way. The grief she was going through was taking a heavy toll on her. Only a few hours earlier she had been blissfully unaware that her life was about to be turned upside down, but now that it had come to pass, she was struggling to accept her fate.

'We will have to spend the rest of the night in the barn,' Zach said. 'Can you walk, or do you want me to carry you?'

'I'll make it,' she said, still not looking in the direction of the house but setting her eyes on the barn instead. 'I know Pa would have wanted me to do the right thing and carry on.'

Emily Fawcett had just gone up even further in Zach's estimation. She was putting on a brave face despite the horrific ordeal she had been put through. How could he not admire her for that? Taking her by the hand and leading her into the dark barn, he felt around on the ledge just inside the door, and when he found the lantern he struck a match and lit it.

The dim light of the kerosene lantern cast an eerie glow around the silent walls of the old barn. With the house cow and her calf gone, the place seemed solemn and forlorn, and it was with a heavy heart that Zach grabbed a pitchfork and fluffed up a stack of hay for the young woman to bed down on. Spying an old horse blanket that the Apache had shunned, he bade Emily lie down on the soft hay and then covered her with the blanket.

'Where are you going to sleep?' she asked.

'I'll fork up a pile of hay and make a bed for myself over by the door.'

She lifted up the blanket. 'You'll do no such thing. There's plenty of room here, and you'll be cold without a blanket over you.'

He hesitated. He didn't really trust himself lying right next to her like that.

'I don't have the patience to argue with you, Zach,' she said sternly. 'You are going to sleep beside me, and that's all there is to it.'

He had to smile at that, then going over to her, lay down and pulled the blanket over the pair of them. She laid her head on his chest and he did nothing to stop her. Nor did he do anything more than place his arm around her when she began to softly cry. He knew there was nothing he could do to ease her sorrow, but at least he could let her know he would stay with her while she went through it.

Hours later, as the dawn's light began to filter through the gaps in the barn's cladding, the harsh reality of what had transpired the night before hit Zach with full force. Jeff was dead, the house was gone, the horses too, and by now the beef as well would have been driven off by the Apache. The young woman sleeping fitfully beside him was now his responsibility and his alone, and not knowing if he had ever had to be responsible for another human being before, and therefore not knowing quite what that entailed, filled him with trepidation.

Getting up quietly so as not to wake Emily, he slipped through the barn door to survey the damage.

A heap of black ash tinged throughout a greyish white was all that was left of the once impressive house. The warmth from the glowing embers still radiated out for a few yards in all directions as he did a circuit of the place. The cellar was completely filled in, and he doubted there would be so much as a scrap of charred bone left of Jeff beneath that lot. It was an ignominious end for the man who had sacrificed his life for this piece of dirt.

He heard a horse whinny, and so his hand instantly went down to close on the butt of his Colt .44. Maybe the Apache hadn't gone too far away after all.

A horse wandered round the side of the barn and then stood there staring at him. It was his own mare – she must have broken away during the night from the bunch the Apache had driven off, and had found her way back. He was relieved. Without a horse they would have been all but stranded here. It would have been a death sentence to travel all the way to Wickenburg on foot.

Just then, Emily emerged from the barn, her hair dishevelled and with wisps of hay sticking out of it. She was completely ashen-faced, but despite that, Zach still thought she was the most beautiful woman he had ever seen.

'He is beneath there somewhere,' she said sadly, as she stared at the spot where the cellar used to be. 'He built this house himself, so I guess he would have wanted to be buried there.' She looked around and sighed. 'I guess there's no future here for me now. This was Pa's dream, not mine. I was happy to go along with it while he was alive, but now he's gone there's no point.'

'There isn't anywhere for you to live anyway,' Zach pointed out. 'It would be miserable living in the barn, and with the horses and cattle all gone, there would be no income to keep you in essentials.'

She turned to him then with what he thought looked like desperation in her eyes. 'Take me to Wickenburg with you.'

He nodded. He had already decided that was the best course of action anyway. He couldn't leave her here alone after what had happened. She wouldn't survive a month before either starvation or the Apache ended her life for her. But he was relieved that she saw it the same way he did. It would have made everything so much more difficult if she had dug her toes in and refused to leave the ranch.

'I'll take the mare into the barn and hook her up to the buckboard,' Zach said. 'Can you get some vegetables from the garden for us to take with us? I'm afraid that's all we're going to have to eat between here and Wickenburg.'

While Emily was off salvaging some carrots and whatever else she could find, Zach caught the mare, and taking her into the barn, set to work harnessing her up. She hadn't pulled a wagon such a long distance before, but she wasn't a total stranger to the job. She had pulled this very same wagon on the ranch when carting fencing gear, so Zach knew she would perform the task well enough, even if she wouldn't be too happy about it.

He had just finished everything and thrown an old canvas and the horse blanket into the wagon on top of a load of hay when Emily came through the barn door with her arms full of fresh produce.

'I worked hard on that garden,' she said despondently. 'It's going to be sad to leave it behind to become overgrown and knowing all that food is going to go to waste.'

He helped her pile the vegetables in the bottom of the wagon. 'It can't be helped, I'm afraid. You're going

60

to have to start a new life someplace else. When we get to Wickenburg we'll try to find a buyer for the ranch so you'll at least have some money to get you started.'

'And what will you do when you get there?'

'I'll see you settled before I move on,' he promised, and then fancied he saw sadness in her eyes at the revelation he wouldn't be hanging around. 'I'm not too sure what I'm going to do for a job yet, or even where I'm going to end up. That bible of mine mentions that I had been in Helena in Montana, and that the citizens thought highly enough of me to present me with a bible, so maybe that's where my future should lie.'

'Helena is a long way away from here,' she said dejectedly.

'That it is. But I'm willing to bet I'd get some answers as to who I really am if I went back there.' He helped Emily up on to the buckboard before climbing up beside her and navigating the wagon through the open door of the barn.

'Do you think the Apache are still out there?' she asked, as they passed the burnt remains of the house, her eyes taking in the spot where her father had lost his life for the final time.

'They'll be revelling in their newfound wealth, I figure. I don't think they'll be out on any more raids for a while, so I'd be surprised if we run across them between here and Wickenburg.'

'Why do they do it, Zach?'

'The Apache?'

She nodded.

61

'White men have pushed them off their ancestral lands, Emily. They are a people without a future, and they blame the white man for that.'

'Do they have to kill people they haven't even met before?' She was thinking of her poor dear pa.

'Whites have killed plenty of their people in the past. Not just men either. Women and even children have been killed.'

She shuddered. 'Who could be barbaric enough to kill an innocent child?'

'Man is a strange creature, Emily. There isn't much he isn't prepared to do when he's motivated by either greed or hatred, and most times that hatred is ill placed.'

'And is it ill placed where the Apache are concerned?' She was hoping to find some reason to hate them for taking her pa's life.

'There have been bad things done on both sides. Let's just say that none of us has behaved how our Creator wished us to.'

She went quiet then, and for the next few miles there was only the sound of the buckboard's wheels on the hard ground and the breathing of the mare to disturb the silence of the early morning.

That evening they camped by a small spring that bubbled up out of the ground beside a rocky outcrop, its water so cool and sweet that Zach doubted he had ever tasted better. He slept that night with one eye open and an ear to the wind, not fully confident that the Apache wouldn't be somewhere nearby. Next morning he was up and getting things ready for travel before the dawn's light had stolen across the ground to wake up Emily.

'You should have woken me,' she said, when she finally opened her eyes and saw he had already organized everything. 'I would have given you a hand with it all.'

'I figured you needed your sleep after everything you've been through. Besides, we've a long journey ahead of us today, and that I'm afraid is going to tire you out.'

Hurriedly getting up, she packed her bedding into the wagon, and then took her place on the seat beside him. 'I'll be more prompt tomorrow morning, I promise,' she said, and then handed him a couple of carrots for him to breakfast on.

Zach studied the horizon as he munched on the carrots. With any luck they would reach Wickenburg before nightfall tomorrow. He would immediately make enquiries in town as to selling the ranch, and would wait around to see the deal go through. After that he might just head to Tombstone and see if he could find work for a few months. If he could get a little money saved up he could travel back to Helena and find out what he needed to know about his past. Only then would he be able to face the future.

They reached Wickenburg without incident. Despite the fact that neither of them had bathed in days, and that Emily had cried on and off for her pa throughout the entire journey, making her eyes red and puffy, nor brushed her glorious mane of hair, Zach still thought she looked stunning. She was a natural beauty who just demanded a

man's admiration without needing to try. He was going to
be mighty sad when the time came to say goodbye to her.

Zach wasted no time in making enquiries as to who might
be interested in buying the ranch, and came up with the
names of two men who owned large spreads not too far
away from the Fawcett ranch. Jeff Fawcett's place would
provide ideal winter grazing for either of them. He had no
illusions as to getting a top price for the place. It was going
to boil down to getting whatever he could, and given the
fact that the ranch was in the path of marauding Apache,
and no longer had a house on it, he figured that price was
going to be a fraction of what its true worth was as grazing
land. But at least Emily would be getting something out of
selling the place, and that would help her in rebuilding
her life here in Wickenburg. While he was waiting for an
offer to materialize he took on whatever work he could
find to keep himself and Emily in food and lodgings.

Just over six weeks later a rancher offered a price for
the parcel of land that Zach thought was more than rea-
sonable, given the circumstances, and so with Emily's permission, he sold the Fawcett ranch to the man, who went
by the name of John Weyden. With everything done and
dusted, and Emily with the money she needed to start a
new life for herself, Zach decided it was time for him to
say goodbye to the young woman he had all but fallen in
love with.

SEVEN

'You're leaving?' Emily asked incredulously.

He nodded, 'First thing tomorrow morning.'

'Why, Zach?' she sounded hurt, as if he was somehow being disloyal.

'I need to find out about myself, Emily. My memory hasn't come back and so I'm going to head to Tombstone to earn enough money to travel back to Helena. I'm sure there are people in Montana who know who I am and can fill in the missing years for me.'

He could see by the expression on her face that she understood his desire to discover his origins, even if she didn't particularly like the fact that he had decided to leave her.

'Take me with you,' she said suddenly, her big green eyes looking up at him beseechingly.

'You need somewhere to call home, and I can't give you that. Dang it, Emily, I don't even know where home is for me.'

'Together we can find out,' she said, hoping he would relent and allow her to go with him. When he just looked away and didn't answer, she placed her hand on his fore-arm to grab his attention. 'I have no family left alive now that Pa is dead.' She waited until his eyes had flicked back to hers. 'You are the closest thing to family I have. If you leave without me I'll be all alone.'

How could he turn her down when she was looking at him like that? She looked so lost and lonely that his heart went out to her.

'Take me with you,' she said softly again, her stunning eyes searching his face for the answer she hoped was going to allay her fears.

'It might be dangerous at times, and I'll be living rough most of the time.'

'I don't care, just take me with you.'

'All right, if you're sure that's what you want, then I will.'

She looked relieved. 'I won't hold you back, I promise you I won't.'

He smiled at her then. 'I'm not sure you could even if you tried, Emily Fawcett.'

The next day they left Wickenburg for Tombstone. The two hundred and fifty miles or so in the buckboard was going to be an ordeal Emily hadn't figured on, and Zach suspected she would be regretting her decision to go with him before the week was done – and it didn't help that the skies darkened and torrential rain fell several days out from Wickenburg. Zach had rigged up a canvas to try and keep the worst of it off Emily, but he could see she was suffering from the conditions, even though she never once complained to him about it.

When they finally trundled into Tombstone weeks later, gaunt and worse for wear, Zach had to marvel at the fact that although the elements had thrown everything they possibly could at Emily Fawcett, not once during the journey had they managed to break either her spirit or her determination to see this adventure through.

Zach found himself a job in a silver mine, and although he hated it, having never worked below ground before, he stuck at it, grimly resolved to make what money he needed to make it to Montana, and still have enough left to live on when he got there. Emily kept offering to give him some of the money from the sale of the ranch, but he just as often declined. The last thing he wanted was for her to spend the money she should be keeping to rebuild her life on helping him.

Zach was in Tombstone for just over three weeks when an incident occurred that eventually led to him being left in no doubt that his future was going to be anything but peaceful. He had finished work for the day and had slipped into a saloon to enjoy a cool beer when a man sidled up to him at the bar, and took a good long look at him.

'Is there something I can help you with?' Zach asked curtly, irritated that the fellow was scrutinizing his face so thoroughly.

'Ain't you Clint Hogan?'

'Not the last time I looked in the mirror.'

'You look mighty like him to me.' He turned to look at a table of cowboys playing poker. 'Hey, Wade, come here and tell me who this feller looks like.'

With a scraping of chair legs, Wade got up from the table and sauntered over for a look.

'What do you reckon?' the first man asked, nodding his head in Zach's direction.

Zach noted the surprised look on Wade's face. 'Why, if that ain't Clint Hogan I'll eat my hat.'

'You'd best get out the salt and pepper then,' Zach said with a bored tone, ''cos my name's Zach Thompson.'

'Well, all I can say to that is that you're a dead ringer for Clint Hogan if ever I've seen one,' Wade stated firmly, 'and I've seen the feller plenty of times before to know exactly what he looks like. You even sound like him.'

'Well, I can't help that. I reckon this is a big enough world that we all have more'n one feller who resembles us.'

'Not unless that feller is your identical twin,' Wade insisted. 'Looking like someone is one thing, but being the exact image of him is another thing altogether.'

'Well, like I said, I don't know this Clint Hogan feller you speak of, so how about you two head on back to your card game and let me finish my drink in peace.'

'I ain't about to argue the toss with Clint Hogan,' Wade said quietly. 'Come on, Jake, let's leave him be before we find ourselves in a whole heap of trouble.'

'I ain't Clint Hogan,' Zach said again as they made a move towards their table.

'Whatever you say, Mr Hogan,' Wade said, and then quickened his pace to rejoin his friends and excitedly tell them about his meeting with none other than Clint Hogan.

Zach went back to sipping his beer as he leaned against the bar. Who in tarnation was Clint Hogan, and why did those two hombres confuse him for this man? As he twisted his head around to look at the table the two men had returned to, he caught every man sitting there staring closely at him, and he began to wonder if coming in here for a quiet beer had been a big mistake. What if word went around Tombstone that this Clint Hogan feller was in town and from now on everyone accosted him on the street thinking he really was the man in question? Nope, he had come to Tombstone hoping to remain as anonymous as he could, staying only long enough to make enough money to get himself and Emily to Helena, and that was the way he wanted it to stay. Clint Hogan or not, he wasn't going to bother getting into any pointless arguments with strangers over the matter, and that was all there was to it. Finishing his beer he walked out of the saloon, but with several pairs of eyes following him as he went.

****

Zach figured the township of Tombstone had to be the roughest place on earth, and so early on he took to wearing the old Colt .44 strapped to his hip wherever he went. If anyone tried to jump him he was going to be ready for them, and if they ended up with a belly full of lead trying to rob him then he wasn't going to lose any sleep over it. Nope, Zach Thompson didn't much care for the type of men who had made Tombstone their home, and he couldn't say he thought much more of the women, either.

Wearing that six-gun ended up being a wise move, as was borne out a few days after the incident in the saloon. He was looking in the window of a gun shop at the rifles on display, hoping to soon have enough spare money to purchase one, as his Winchester had been lost when the house went up in flames that fateful night at the ranch, when a man in the street below the boardwalk began to holler loudly. Abandoning his window shopping he turned round to see what all the commotion was about.

'Yep, you!' the fellow shouted, his finger pointing right at Zach.

Zach just stared at him in mute silence as the stranger stepped closer to the boardwalk, glaring up at Zach with undisguised hatred in his eyes.

'I've waited a long time to run into you. Now that I have, you ain't gunna walk away like you did when you gunned my brother down.'

'Mister, I don't have any idea what you're talking about.'

'The hell you don't. I'm Bill Jackson, Joel Jackson's brother. You gunned him down in Abilene three years back and I swore I'd make you pay for it, and now I'm gunna do just that.'

The man's gun hand was hovering very close to the butt of the Army Colt that dangled on his hip, too close for Zach's liking, and the way he wore his gun spoke of the fact that he made his living pulling it out fast.

'You've mistaken me for somebody else, mister,' Zach said, his heart beating rapidly in his chest, despite him appearing outwardly calm.

'I'd know you anywhere, Hogan. Your face is etched on my memory for all time.'

There was that name again. Just who was this Clint Hogan character that was causing him so much grief? 'Look, I have no quarrel with you. I'm not this … Clint Hogan feller everyone seems to think I am. I've never heard of the man in my life.'

The man in the street below him sneered up at Zach. 'Well, that's an outright lie. Everyone's heard of Clint Hogan.'

'Well I haven't,' Zach said in exasperation. 'Who's he supposed to be?'

'Only the fastest man alive with a gun,' a man shouted out from amongst the crowd that was gathering to watch events unfold.

'The fastest next to me,' Jackson corrected him. 'Hang around, all of you, you're about to see the great Clint Hogan laid in the dust.'

'This has gone far enough!' Zach exploded. 'I've had all I'm gunna take of this Clint Hogan nonsense. My name is Zachariah Thompson, and I most definitely am not a fast gun.'

'I'm done with talking,' Jackson said, taking a couple of steps backwards and flexing the fingers on his gun hand in readiness.

'You're pure loco,' Zach said desperately, seeing where all this was heading, but feeling powerless to stop it.

'Loco enough to see you dead, you piece of scum.'

'Somebody get the sheriff,' Zach implored. 'This feller's bent on causing trouble.'

'You'd better believe it, Hogan, and the trouble is gunna be all yours. Now, reach for your shooting iron.'

'I'm not interested in drawing on you, mister, and that's all there is to it.'

'Then you leave me with no choice, because I'm not gunna let you walk away from this. I owe it to Joel to put you in the ground.'

'This is madness!'

Bill Jackson was done talking. His Army Colt was going to do his speaking from here on in, and as his hand swept up to grasp his six-gun, Zach's own hand reacted without any prompting from his reluctant brain, the .44 springing free of its holster with a speed that spoke of pure class.

Jackson's Army Colt cleared his cut-down holster, but that was as far as the contest progressed in his favour, for the old .44 roared in Zach's hand and Bill Jackson copped the full brunt of its fury.

Zach Thompson watched on in horror as Jackson took two steps backwards, a patch of crimson rapidly staining the front of his new store-bought shirt. He looked up at Zach with incomprehension in his eyes. It was as if he couldn't quite believe he had been out-gunned.

'I didn't want to,' Zach said frantically. 'If only you had left things alone, then this wouldn't have happened.'

Jackson teetered on the spot for a moment, aware that when he went down then his life would be forfeit. But even with the strongest will in the world he couldn't cheat death, and seconds later he pitched face forward into the street at the foot of the boardwalk, just as dead as dead could be.

'What's going on here?' A man was forcing his way through the crowd, and from his elevated position up on the boardwalk, Zach could see a metal star on his shirt glinting in the sunlight as he progressed.

'The feller standing up there just shot this feller, Sheriff,' a man said, as Tombstone's law officer finally arrived on the scene.

Sheriff Ben Cookson looked up at Zach with deep suspicion in his pale blue eyes. 'What did you go and do that for?'

'He drew on me,' Zach said in exasperation. 'He kept saying I was some feller who had killed his brother, and he wouldn't let it drop.'

'And did you?'

'Did I what?'

'Kill his brother?'

'No!'

'That's Clint Hogan standing up there on the boardwalk, Sheriff,' the same man from the crowd said again.

Zach would have loved to have belted the fellow right on his prominent snout for saying that. Things had got too far out of hand as it was, without him telling lies to stir things up even more.

73

The sheriff's eyes returned to Zach. 'That right, mister, are you Clint Hogan?'

'No, I am not!' Zach said firmly, and not without a certain amount of anger.

'He sure looks like him to me, Sheriff.'

'Who started the ruckus?'

'The dead feller did, Sheriff. He called Hogan out and wasn't gunna let it go until they traded lead. He went for his gun first, but Hogan was too fast for him.'

'I am *not* this Clint Hogan feller!' Zach growled throatily. 'Why won't anybody listen to me?'

Cookson pushed his Stetson back from his forehead as he gazed down at the dead man. 'Well, Clint Hogan or not, I can't arrest him for defending himself.' He transferred his attention to Zach now. 'But if there's any more trouble because of you, then I'm gunna take a mighty dim view of it.'

'Tell *them* that, not me,' Zach's hand did a wide sweep of those who were standing in the street watching events unfold. 'All I want is to be left alone to mind my own business, but they seem hell-bent on claiming I'm somebody else, so they can pick a quarrel with me.'

'I usually find that if a feller is attracting that kind of attention it's because he's done something to deserve it,' Cookson answered abruptly.

'Well, not this time, Sheriff.'

Cookson eyeballed him for a moment. 'You're free to go, Hogan, but mind what I've just told you.'

'I am *not* Clint Hogan!' Zach thundered, getting angrier by the second.

'Just go before I arrest you for disturbing the peace!'

Zach could see he wasn't going to persuade anyone that he was just plain old Zachariah Thompson and not Clint Hogan, and so full of dejection he strode off down the boardwalk towards the boarding house to tell Emily about the torrid time he had just had.

EIGHT

'Why do they keep thinking you are this Clint Hogan person?' Emily asked when Zach had told her about what had happened with Bill Jackson out in the street.

'Apparently I look so much like him that folks can't tell the difference. It's just my luck to be mistaken for a gunfighter.'

'You don't think you could be related to him, do you?'

Zach looked at her thoughtfully for a moment. 'I hadn't thought of that, but maybe that explains it. Maybe he's a cousin or something. The trouble is, with this dang memory of mine refusing to come back I've really got no way of knowing.'

'Maybe we'll get the answers to that when we go to Helena.'

'Look, Emily, don't you think it's time we went our separate ways? I agreed to bring you to Tombstone because you were grieving for your pa, and so I didn't want to leave you in Wickenburg to cope on your own. But this can't go on forever. You have to make a life for yourself sooner or later.'

She stared down at her shoes for a moment, and when she looked back at him he saw sadness in her pretty eyes. 'Do you not like me, Zach?'

He was lost for words for what seemed to be an eternity. 'Of course I like you, Emily,' he said eventually.

'Then why do you keep trying to get rid of me? This isn't the first time you've suggested we part ways.'

'Because ... because ...' he had to think fast – she was standing there with her jaw jutting out, scrutinizing his face to make sure he was going to give her an honest answer. 'It's because we come from different worlds.'

'How do you know?'

'Because ...' he tried to come up with something, but he couldn't really answer that one.

'The truth is, you have no idea what world you come from. Your life from here on in is a blank canvas, and you can make of it whatever you choose to.'

'And if I choose to not have you in my life ... what then?'

'If that is your decision, then I would respect it. But don't try to fob me off with the ridiculous reason for abandoning me that you just have.'

'Why would you even want to stay with me?'

'I've explained that to you before. You are the only thing resembling family that I've got left, and I fell for you only days after Pa brought you home to look after you, so I can't just deny my feelings for you.'

The revelation stunned him.

'Don't look so surprised, Zach. I'm sure you've had women fall in love with you before.'

'I ... I don't remember.'

She laughed at that. 'I guess that should make me happy. At least I'll have no past loves to compete with.'

'After today you won't be safe with me. I don't know how many men there are out there who have a beef with Clint Hogan. That puts you in danger.'

'I don't care. I just want to be with you, Zach.'

'I'll give the matter some thought.'

'That's all I ask. But make your decision based on your feelings for me, and not anything else. I'm a big girl, and I can handle hardships just as well as anyone else can.'

She walked away from him then, leaving him to ponder her words and marvel at what a truly remarkable woman she really was. What she saw in him he would never know, but he would be lying if he claimed he wasn't pleased that she had confessed she was in love with him.

He didn't really need to think about whether he would take her with him when he left for Helena. He was more than a little in love with her as it was, and so the thought of leaving her behind and never seeing her again didn't sit well with him at all. Then, of course, if she was in love with him as she claimed to be, he would be a fool to turn her away. What man in his right mind would spurn the advances of a woman like Emily Fawcett?

She would make a fine wife if it came to that, and it just might, once he had sorted out this problem of who he was. He might very well be ready to settle down and raise a crop of kids once he had come to his right frame of mind again, and he couldn't think of anyone he would rather be sharing his bed with than Emily.

****

Another two weeks went by, with Zach having to endure the stares and pointed fingers of the residents of Tombstone every time he walked down the street. The name *Clint Hogan* was never far from their lips let alone their thoughts, and he thought he would go crazy if one more person asked him how many men he had gunned down. It seemed no one bought his explanation that he was anybody more than just plain old Zachariah Thompson, and no amount of insisting from him that he was would ever change their minds on that score.

Fifteen days to the day that he had been forced to kill Bill Jackson, two men turned up in Tombstone asking folks as to the whereabouts of Clint Hogan. The news of it reached Zach's ears courtesy of Charlie Bonner, a bartender in one of Tombstone's many saloons, and the revelation sent a wave of fear coursing through Zach. He just knew they were here to give him trouble, and he was at his wits' end trying to figure out a way he could avoid it.

Avoiding trouble seemed to be impossible for Zach though, and less than twenty-four hours after he had been informed of the arrival of the strangers they had tracked him down, knocking loudly on the door to his room at the boarding house with a vigour that spoke of their evil intent towards him.

Zach just knew if he opened that door he would be in trouble, so he was glad Emily wasn't here. She was in her own room at the end of the landing, and hadn't dropped by to see him today as yet. He hoped she would stay in her room, too, as he had no wish for her to get mixed up in all of this.

Taking the .44 off the dresser beside the bed he stood to one side of the door and waited for the pounding to stop. 'Who is it?' he demanded gruffly.

'Just open the door, Hogan!'

'My name isn't Hogan. Tell me who you are and what you want.'

'Stop playing silly games with us, Hogan. We want to know where the money is, and we ain't gunna leave until you tell us.'

'I'm not Clint Hogan, and I don't know anything about any money.' He made a move for the open window. If he could get down to the street and come back up the stairs undetected he might be able to surprise them. Getting the drop on them might just get him some of the answers to this riddle that he so desperately needed. He was just slipping through the window when he heard the door knob rattling.

'We haven't got all day, Hogan, so unlock this door.'

With the agility bestowed upon him due to his youth, Zach Thompson dropped to the street from his second-storey window, landing on his feet but instantly feeling the impact in his hips. 'I'm gunna pay for that tomorrow morning,' he muttered to himself as he made his way round to the front door of the boarding house.

He could hear two men discussing what was to be done as he crept catlike up the stairs.

'How we gunna get him to open the door?' one fellow said in a low tone.

'Well, Zeb, I figure we could smash the door down.'

'That'd be like committing suicide. You know how good he is with a gun. We'd both be full of holes before we got more'n three feet inside that room.'

'Maybe we should just wait him out. He has to come out of there some time.'

'No need to wait, boys,' Zach said calmly, the old Colt .44 in his right hand pointing right at them as he left the top tread of the stairs and stood on the landing behind them.

'Now, Clint,' the one named Zeb said quickly, as he raised his hands to show he had no intention of making a play for his gun, 'me an' Steve ain't here for any gunplay.'

'Well just to be on the safe side, how 'bout dropping those gun-belts?'

Two gun-belts fell to the floor of the landing.

'Now, how 'bout telling me what this is all about?'

'Red sent us to find out where the money is.'

'Who is Red, and what money are you talking about?'

'Come on, Clint, stop all this tomfoolery. You know what I'm talking about. Red wants to know where you've stashed the money from the bank job.'

Zach took in each man's appearance. The one named Zeb was tallish, a shade over six feet he figured, with an impressive moustache as thick and as black as the ace of spades. It matched the colour of his hair perfectly. His grey eyes were keen, not missing a beat. Zach had no doubt he was the cleverer of the two men.

Steve, on the other hand, was much shorter and of a stockier build than his companion. His brown eyes looked almost vacant, as if he wasn't quite all there – and maybe he wasn't, Zach didn't know; after all, he didn't know the pair of them from a bar of soap.

'Suppose you humour me. Tell me who this Red feller is.' The .44 was still pointing right at the pair, and Zeb at least could see that the man holding it wasn't in the mood to be messed around with.

Zeb sighed, 'All right, Clint, we'll play it your way. Red Wilson sent Steve and me here when he heard tell you were in Tombstone. You see, after that bank job, when we got split up on account of the posse that was after us, the money from the bank we knocked over disappeared.'

'And this Red Wilson feller thinks I've got it?'

'Well, it was you who was holding the bag when we all high-tailed it outta that town.'

'I'll tell you what you can do,' Zach said calmly. 'You can tell your boss that not only do I not have the money from his bank job, but I'm not Clint Hogan, either.'

'Now, Clint, you know that Red ain't a feller to be crossed. If'n I take that message back to him he'll come after you, for sure. He's no respecter of fast guns. He'll send several gunnies after you if he has to.'

'How can I get it into your thick head that I am *not* Clint Hogan?'

'I don't know why you're playing this crazy game, Clint. You an' me, we always got on fine, didn't we? I never thought I'd live to see the day you'd try to cheat me out of my share of the loot. I'd never have done that to you, and what's more, you know it, too.'

Zach fancied the hurt look in Zeb's eyes was for real. He honestly thought that this Clint Hogan feller, whom he had considered to be his friend, had betrayed him.

It was Zach's turn to sigh this time. 'I'm gunna try to explain this to you so that you'll understand. So listen up.'

'I hope you will, Clint, 'cos I want to understand, I really do. I don't want to walk away from here believing you deliberately cheated me.'

Zach took a deep breath, and then took his time releasing it before beginning. 'Folks around here are mistaking me for this Clint Hogan feller you speak of,' he said tiredly – he had lost count of the number of times he had felt compelled to explain this – 'but I'm not him. I accept I might look mighty like him. Dang it, I might even look *just* like him. But I can assure you I'm not him. My name is Zachariah Thompson, and I work in one of the silver mines in Tombstone. So not only do I not know anything about any stolen money, I don't know any Red Wilson either. Nor do I know you two hombres.'

Zeb stared silently into Zach's eyes for a while. 'You might be a fast gun, Clint,' he said at last, 'but you ain't gunna be a match for the men Red'll send after you. He's madder than a nest of hornets over what you've done, and I can't say I blame him. Thirty thousand dollars is a lot of money. We've always split the loot evenly, every man getting his share. So doing what you've done doesn't set well with any of us.'

So Zeb hadn't believed a word Zach had just told him. What was it he had to do to convince folks he was who he said he was?

'And what's happened to Tyrell and Harrison? They ain't joined up with the rest of us like they usually do. You ain't had something to do with that, have you?'

Zach groaned. 'I suppose they're fellers I'm meant to know, and you're accusing me of doing away with them.'

'I ain't accusing you of nothing. I was just wondering if you knew what had happened to them, is all. It's kinda strange they didn't turn up to get their share of the loot.' Zeb couldn't disguise the look of suspicion that had crept over his face.

'Pick up your gun-belts and get out of here,' Zach ordered, his patience finally giving out. 'If you come back here bothering me again, then I can promise you it won't end well for you.'

'Steve and me won't be the ones coming back, Clint, you know that. Red'll send some gunnies after you, and it'll be you it doesn't end well for.'

'You just tell this Red hombre he's barking up the wrong tree. I am *not* Clint Hogan.'

'Whatever you say, Clint,' Zeb said sadly, and then carefully bending down, picked up his gun-belt, making sure his hand was nowhere near the pistol that was nestled in the holster. 'Steve an' me'll be moseying along now.'

Zach watched them as they crossed the landing to the stairs, his .44 covering them every step of the way, and he didn't lower it until he heard the front door at the bottom of the stairs open and then bang shut.

NINE

Although Zach hadn't made anywhere near the amount of money he had planned to working in the mine, he figured the prudent thing to do was to get out of Tombstone before Red Wilson sent those gunnies Zeb had mentioned after him. Besides, Emily had insisted they could use some of the money from the sale of the ranch to tide them over if need be, and although Zach hated taking money from her, he reasoned it was the lesser of the two evils if the only other alternative was waiting it out in Tombstone for those gunfighters to arrive.

Zach left Tombstone the day after his altercation with Zeb and Steve, provisioning the buckboard well and getting the blacksmith to rig up some metal ribs on the wagon so he could stretch the well oiled canvas over them that he had bought. This time he was going to make sure he and Emily were protected from the elements if the weather turned bad on them.

They trundled out of Tombstone under the cover of darkness, Zach hoping that no one had seen them go, and confident that no one knew where they were headed. It was going to be an epic journey – at least fourteen hundred miles of rugged terrain lay between Tombstone and Helena – but if Zach was to discover his roots, then Helena was the only place on this earth that it would happen.

They would head for Utah, doing their best to avoid the larger towns where he might be mistaken for Clint Hogan, and from there into Idaho. All things going well he reckoned they should be safe from the vengeful Red Wilson by then, and it would be simple enough to cross over into Montana and make their way to Helena. That was the plan, at any rate, but Zach was wise enough to know that things didn't always go according to plan. If Red Wilson was determined to get back that money from the bank job – and at the moment he seemed to think that Zach had it – then maybe Zach and Emily wouldn't even get out of Arizona before he caught up with them.

Zach had bought another horse while he was in Tombstone. He figured his life and that of Emily's depended upon it. Not only would two pull the wagon a whole heap faster than one, but if one were to go lame then they wouldn't be held up for days waiting for it to come right, always wondering and worrying if Red Wilson was about to show up.

Zach gave the reins a sudden flick. He would push the two mares hard tonight, in an attempt to put as much distance between them and Tombstone as he possibly could. Emily could sleep now, and then in the morning, if the horses still had it in them, they could have a quick break for feed and water, and a short rest, and then Emily could take over while Zach caught up on a few hours' sleep.

He gave some thought to this whole business as Emily settled down under the canvas for what he knew would be an uncomfortable night's sleep – the jerking and jolting of the buckboard over the stony ground would see to that.

Helena was a long way off, and there would be Apache as well as the usual deprivations of the trail to contend with. There was a good chance that Red Wilson wouldn't need to exact his revenge after all. Quite possibly thirst, starvation, heat, cold or Indians would see to that.

He wondered where this Clint Hogan really was. Zeb had mentioned something about two other fellers as well – men going by the names of Tyrell and Harrison, he seemed to remember. Maybe Hogan was in cahoots with them. The three of them had run off with the loot, had maybe even divided it up and then split up. That would be ten thousand dollars apiece, a tidy sum of money indeed. If they had any sense they would have crossed over into Mexico by now, and be well out of reach of Red Wilson, as well as the authorities, who would undoubtedly be after them.

Zach felt a sudden jolt run through him. He hadn't considered that until just now. The authorities would be after Clint Hogan, and because Zach kept being mistaken for the bank robber, that meant they would be after him. Possibly the sheriff back in Tombstone didn't arrest him because Hogan wasn't wanted in Arizona, or maybe he hadn't heard yet that Hogan was even wanted by the law. That kind of news often took months to filter down to all the little towns. But Hogan may well be wanted where Zach was now heading. Dang it, but this whole business was going from bad to worse in less time than it took to skin a coon. He was a wanted man every which way he turned, and from now on he was going to have to be extra vigilant if he wanted to come through this trouble unscathed.

It was just as well he had purchased a new Winchester and shotgun back in Tombstone, along with plenty of shells and cartridges to go with them. He figured he was going to be firing them at much more than just the wild critters they encountered along the trail now that he knew he had so many human enemies. He didn't fancy tangling with the law, but given the fact he hadn't been able to convince a single soul back in Tombstone that he wasn't Clint Hogan, he figured that if he didn't want to hang for a crime he hadn't committed, he would have no option but to preserve his freedom with a gun in his hand.

Zach lifted the canvas flap to check on Emily, and was surprised to see she was already asleep. How she could have drifted off so quickly, especially given the rough treatment she must be getting back there, was a mystery to him. She was an unusual woman, that was for sure, and he worried about being in such close company with her on this long journey. He was a man, after all, and she a beautiful and desirable young woman. He wasn't sure how he would control the urges when they came on, and he was certain they would from time to time. Just looking at her was enough to set him off if he didn't watch himself closely.

She was very trusting of him, and he just hoped that trust wouldn't prove to be misplaced. He really didn't know what he was capable of. He had already killed several men. He had handled his six-gun like a true professional, which had surprised nobody more than him. He obviously wasn't the man he had thought he was when it came to using a gun. So maybe he wasn't the man he thought he was with women, either. He hoped for Emily's sake that his amnesia wasn't hiding a propensity to take what he wanted when it came to the opposite sex. If it was, then his true nature might just reveal itself before the journey was over, and there would be nobody on hand to save the young woman from his unwanted advances.

Zach shuddered, and it wasn't because the cold night air was closing in on him. He really hoped he wasn't that kind of man, especially where Emily was concerned. She was something special, and he wanted her to love him for himself, and not come to fear and hate him as some kind of brute beast.

Making a conscious effort to push the young woman out of his mind, he directed his thoughts to the way he had handled that old Colt .44 that was strapped to his hip. Twice now he had displayed unusual prowess with it. The first time was out at the Fawcett ranch when the two drifters had breezed in and were threatening Jeff and Emily. He had reached for that six-gun and dispensed justice with it in the blink of an eye. The speed with which he had sent hot lead screaming out of the barrel of the worn firearm had startled him more than anybody, and it had left him wondering where he had picked up that skill.

Then, of course, there was the shooting of the young man in the main street of Tombstone, just a few days back. Although it had been obvious the fellow was a gunfighter by the way he carried his shooting iron, he had been no match for Zach, with that .44 fair leaping into his hand when the kid had made a play for his gun. It had been all over so fast that Zach hadn't even had a chance to think it through before he had acted. Pure instinct had taken over and directed the entire thing for him, merely leaving him to ponder in the aftermath of it how he had come to be so proficient at something he had no memory of ever having mastered. When push came to shove, Zachariah Thompson was an accomplished killer, on a par with the best gunfighters money could hire.

Zach woke Emily just as the sun crested the horizon the following morning, and with an exhortation to wake him immediately should she spot anyone approaching, he handed her the reins and gratefully slipped under the blankets in the wagon for a well deserved sleep. He was so dog tired that the jolting of the buckboard didn't seem to bother him, and he soon felt himself slipping into a world of blackness, his senses dead to everything that was going on around him.

****

A man was suddenly standing before him. He was tall and pushing seventy, but Zach couldn't get a good look at him, as his face was obscured by the gloom that surrounded him. He was saying something that Zach couldn't quite make out. Something about a man keeping his word, and how it meant more to him than anything else. But that was the only bit of his speech that Zach picked up. The rest was just a mass of garbled sounds that produced no effect other than leaving Zach confused.

The man disappeared, and now a woman stepped through the veil of darkness, her face downcast, as if she carried the weight of the world upon her shoulders. She was a pretty woman, about twenty-five or thereabouts, her long auburn hair splayed in wild abandon, framing her pale face, making her appearance all the more melancholy. *'Don't go down that path, my love,'* she said sadly. *'Many a man has, and it has been the ruin of every single one of them.'*

Then she was gone, her face and form melted back into the gloom almost as quickly as she had appeared, leaving Zach grasping for her, desperate to bring her back, his heart beating faster than it ever had before with the fear that he would never see her again.

Zachariah Thompson woke up in a cold sweat. His heart was pounding and his pulse was racing. He had no idea who the young beauty was who had come to him in his dream, but he sensed that she was an integral part of him, a part that he had somehow lost somewhere along the way, and wished he could have back again, but knew he never could.

Emily twisted around in her seat and peeped in through the flap. 'I was hoping to give you another hour or so before I woke you. You've only had three hours sleep.'

He sat up and waited for the grogginess to flee from his head. 'I'll be all right,' he said eventually. 'It's the horses we have to see to now. They'll need to rest for three or four hours before we push on.'

'Do you want me to pull up?'

He nodded. 'As soon as I'm fully awake I'll unhitch them and see that they get watered and fed.'

'And I'll see to rustling up some breakfast,' she promised, before pulling back on the reins to let the two mares know their obligation was over, for the time being at least.

'Do you think they have come after us?' Emily asked later on, as she handed Zach a plate of fried potato slices and bacon.

'No. I don't think anybody'll know we're gone yet. It'll take a while for Zeb and Steve to report back to Red, and then a day or so before Red sends anyone out after us.' What he didn't tell her was that the law in the town the money had been stolen from would have been hunting for Clint Hogan all along, and were bound to have heard that he was in Tombstone. It would only be a matter of time before they sent someone there to check out the validity of the report, and once satisfied he had been there, would immediately send someone after him, bounty hunters maybe.

'Zach …' she began tentatively, as she passed him a steaming cup of coffee, 'are we in danger out here from the Apache?'

'I don't think so,' he lied, not wishing to cause her the type of ongoing anxiety that might make her crack from the strain somewhere further down the trail. A woman who went to pieces out in the wilderness was a handicap no man should have to cope with. Besides, he had no idea where the Apache were at the moment. They might still be somewhere in Arizona, or they might have crossed over into Mexico for a spell. After all, they seemed just as happy to raid the Mexicans on the other side of the Rio Grande as they did the ranches and small settlements on this side of the river. But he couldn't afford to worry about them himself at the moment – his number one priority was putting as much distance between himself and Tombstone as quickly as he could.

Zach hobbled the horses so they wouldn't wander too far away, and then settled down in the shade of a tree for another couple of hours' sleep. When Emily woke him he would round up the horses, hitch them to the wagon and head off once again, trusting to providence that they would be keeping one step ahead of those who wished him dead.

Two hours later, Emily roused him from his deep slumber, a slumber that thankfully hadn't produced the vivid dreams he had experienced earlier. Getting to his feet, he bent over just long enough to scoop up his bedroll and stash it in the wagon before heading off to gather in the horses.

They hadn't wandered off far. There was plenty of rough grass thereabouts for them to graze on, so they had stayed close by, heads down and cropping the coarse vegetation as if their very lives depended on it, consuming as much as they could in as short a time as possible. Leading them back to the buckboard, he set to work hitching them to the wagon.

He kept his eyes constantly on the alert when they finally rolled off. There were a hundred and one places for the Apache to conceal themselves in the territory they were currently travelling through. He had his Winchester fully loaded and laid at his feet, and the shotgun within easy reach just inside the flap should either of them be needed – though God forbid that they ever would be.

That evening as Emily slept, Zach took the opportunity presented by the tranquillity of the night, to try and piece together what he had found out about the situation he found himself in.

Red Wilson was the head honcho of a gang of bank robbers, which seemed fairly certain from what Zeb had told him. Clint Hogan, whom everyone and his uncle seemed to think was who Zach really was, must be a member of Red's gang, or at least he was until he disappeared with the thirty thousand dollars in loot that the gang had stolen from the last bank they had struck.

Tyrell and Harrison had disappeared as well, which seemed to indicate to Zach that they were in on the whole thing with Hogan. If they had any sense at all the three of them would be in Mexico, cooling their heels and waiting for the furore to die down. Two or three years south of the border ought to take the heat off so they could come back and pick up their lives as much wealthier men, under assumed names, naturally.

Of course, Clint Hogan being in Mexico for that length of time didn't help Zach Thompson out one little bit. With the real Clint Hogan having gone to ground, and in another country no less, no one was going to believe that he was Zach when he was the spitting image of Hogan. So it was a classic case of Hogan committing the crime, but Zach doing the time, or being forced to go on the run, as it were.

He really was caught between a rock and a hard place, and only the good folks of Helena in Montana would be able to extricate him from it. If they could positively identify him as being Zachariah Thompson, the man they had presented a bible to, *for services rendered to the citizens of Helena*, then this nightmare that had been thrust upon him would finally go away.

The inscription inside that bible had said the book had been presented to him in 1878. It was now 1881. There should be plenty of souls still living in Helena who had known him well and would be willing to come to his defence, if only he could get there before either Red Wilson or the law got to him. He sure was the unluckiest feller alive. Fancy being mistaken for a notorious gun-fighter, and one who was not only wanted by the law, but also by the very outlaws he had ridden with. Why couldn't he have resembled someone of substance, someone who would have commanded respect for all the right reasons? But no, he had to look like a feller the whole world was against. Sometimes life just wasn't fair.

TEN

They had been shadowing Zach for the past two hours now, a small group of riders staying way off to the west but keeping pace with the wagon. They weren't close enough for Zach to determine how many of them there were, but he had no doubt they had spotted the white canvas covering the buckboard, and were just waiting for an opportune time to pay an impromptu visit.

He and Emily were twelve days out from Tombstone now, and in a particularly wild and unpopulated section of Arizona, so whoever it was out there were either Apache, or they were white men sent to apprehend Clint Hogan. Either way a man looked at it, the situation spelled trouble with a capital T.

Emily had noticed his eyes constantly flicking off in the direction of the riders. 'Is there something troubling you, Zach?' she asked as she sat beside him on the buckboard.

He sighed. 'I was hoping to keep it from you a little longer,' he confessed, 'because I didn't want to alarm you unnecessarily, but we have company off to your right.'

Emily Fawcett's young eyes scanned the horizon. 'Are they here for us?' she asked nervously.

'I suspect they are,' he admitted.

'Apache …?'

'I don't know yet. They may be, or they may be Red Wilson's men, or even the law.' He swallowed hard. 'Out of the three I'm hoping it's the law. I reckon they're the only ones who won't kill us.'

'Why are they staying so far off?'

'They're biding their time, waiting for their opportunity to catch us at a vulnerable moment.'

'Do you think they're waiting for dark?'

He nodded. He would have just pressed on through the night if the horses had been up to it. That would have made it harder for whoever it was to strike unexpectedly. But the horses were already tired from a long day's trek, and if he pushed them any harder he risked ruining them, and reaching Helena would be impossible if that happened.

'I think we'll make camp early for a change,' he said, suddenly pulling back on the reins. While he still had some daylight he could get things organized so he could put up a spirited defence.

She looked at him in alarm. 'Is that wise? Won't that make it easier for them to catch up with us?'

'They would have caught up with us anyway, Emily. I'd rather meet them on my terms than theirs.'

She didn't argue. She had to concede that he knew more about these things than she did. If he thought it best to put up a fight from the spot they were in now, then she would do all that was within her power to assist him.

Zach unhitched the horses and tied them to the wagon. Grabbing a bucket he filled it from the barrel of water he had brought along and let the first mare slake her thirst before refilling it and giving the grey mare her turn. He hated using up his precious supply like this, but he really had no choice. Although he was sure they would have found water no more than an hour or so ahead, he couldn't risk it. He had to use the last hour of light to prepare for when those men came riding in. Hopefully they would come across water tomorrow and he could top up the barrel again.

He pulled a couple of armloads of sweet-smelling hay from the pile he had in the wagon. He had bought it from the livery man back in Tombstone just before they left. The reasoning being it would not only serve for bedding, but also for emergency rations for the two mares. He gave it to them now, and then leaving them to it, began his preparations to stave off an attack. Looking towards the horizon he noted that the men who had been following him had also stopped.

As soon as it got dark he would get Emily to bed down in the wagon, while he crawled underneath and kept watch. When they came creeping in, which would probably be in the early hours of the morning, he would be ready for them, ready to give them both barrels of the shotgun as well as a few rounds from his trusty .44 if it was required.

The sun was sinking fast, and just before it sank too low to cast sufficient light to see any great distance, Zach checked out the position of the riders. They had moved in a little closer since he had brought the buckboard to a halt more than three-quarters of an hour ago. He could see three horses with their heads down and grazing. He could also see a thin plume of smoke rising straight up into the rapidly darkening sky; they were obviously cooking their evening meal, biding their time until the hour came to act.

Zach settled down beneath the wagon and waited patiently. With the last feeble rays of the sun dying away the air had suddenly cooled rapidly, and so he pulled the old army blanket he had with him around his shoulders to stave off the cold, and wondered how many men he was going to have to contend with.

The hours passed slowly by, and Zach's eyelids began to grow heavier with each passing minute. Sometime after two o'clock in the morning, just as he was beginning to think he couldn't stay awake a moment longer, a noise somewhere out there in the dark snapped him to attention. It wasn't a loud noise – more like the sound a man's boot makes when it dislodges a small piece of rock.

Sleep fled from Zach's eyes as a shot of pure adrenalin coursed through his body. They had finally arrived, and were approaching the camp on foot, no doubt hoping to catch Zach slumbering, and if they had just waited another half an hour they might well have succeeded.

The first dark shape came into view as it glided past the still glowing embers of the campfire: it was making for the buckboard. Zach knew there would be others, but right at this moment he didn't know where. Maybe they had surrounded the wagon and were approaching from all directions. Whatever the tactic they had decided to employ, he had to act against this particular feller, and act now before he reached the wagon.

'Halt right there!' Zach hollered, his shotgun pointed right at the man.

A bullet smashed into the wheel of the buckboard not more than a dozen inches from Zach's head, so he had no choice but to pull the trigger and blast the intruder back into the remnants of the fire. Instinct told him to roll over and cover the other side of the wagon, and he didn't do it a moment too soon. A bullet kicked up a small pile of stones beside him, so aiming the scattergun in the direction he fancied the shot had come from, he pulled the second trigger.

A grunt came back at him from the dark space beyond the buckboard, and then a heavy thump as a man's body made contact with the ground. That was one less threat he had to worry about.

He wriggled out from under the wagon. They knew where he was now, and so if he stayed he would be nothing more than a sitting duck. Abandoning the shotgun, he pulled his Colt .44 clear of its holster, and crouching down a short distance from the wagon, listened carefully for any sounds that might betray his attackers' whereabouts.

'Zach … Zach …'

Dang it, it was Emily calling him. If he answered he would betray his position and whoever it was who was gunning for him would make pretty short work of it.

'Zach ... Zach ...' she called again.

He must ignore her plaintive cries and remain where he was if there was going to be any chance of surviving this. He heard a muffled cry and then a scuffling before everything went quiet.

'I have the woman, Hogan!' a deep and infinitely threatening male voice pierced the darkness several yards to the right of the wagon. 'If you don't show yourself I'm gunna be forced to put a bullet in her head.'

Zach groaned. If only she had stayed put and not called out, then everything would have been all right.

'Not gunna tell you again, Hogan. You've got ten seconds to present yourself or your woman is gunna die!'

Well, that was it then. The game was up. He had made a good fist of it, but there was nothing for it but to do as he had been ordered, and hope that mercy would be extended towards both himself and Emily.

'All right,' he said, slipping the .44 back in his holster, 'I'll do as you say.'

Expecting to cop a bullet in the chest any second he moved cautiously, and not without a certain amount of foreboding, towards the man who held Emily hostage.

'You're one slippery fish, Hogan,' the man said when Zach came to stand in front of him. 'Red is madder than a bear robbed of her cubs over what you've done. And now you've shot Ted and Hal. I suppose they're both dead?'

'I haven't checked them. But they left me with no choice. They fired at me first.'

'They'll be dead, for sure. I've never known you to miss before, especially with a shotgun. But you did have a choice. You had the choice not to rob us blind of that loot. Now, where is it? If you tell me, I'll let you and your woman go.'

Like hell you will, Zach thought to himself. When he told the man he didn't have the money, he figured the feller had Red's orders to kill Zach on the spot. Even if he actually did have the money and handed it over, he doubted he would have been allowed to live. He must figure out a way to prolong this so he could work himself into a position to disarm the man and so turn the tables.

'What makes you think I'd be carrying thirty thousand dollars on me?'

'For your sake you'd better be.'

Zach couldn't see the fellow's face clearly in the dark, but his voice sounded vaguely familiar. He felt sure he must have met the man somewhere before, but of course he couldn't remember.

'Harrison and Tyrell have it,' he said, trying to sound calm, despite the slight trembling his legs were experiencing as his brain told him he was most likely about to die.

'And where are they?'

'I don't know.'

The hammer clicked back on the six-gun the man had pointed right at Emily's head. 'Not good enough, Hogan!' he said sharply. 'You've got just two seconds left before I pull this trigger.'

103

'Wait!' Zach said quickly, 'I'll tell you.'

'Where is it?'

'It's in the wagon. It's in a tin beneath a pile of hay.'

'You'd better not be fooling with me,' the man warned. 'You've messed me about enough as it is, and that's something I don't forget in a hurry.'

'It's there,' Zach lied.

'All right, then we're gunna move over to the wagon nice and slow. Any sudden movements and this one gets it.' He ground the barrel of his pistol into Emily's temple, eliciting a little gasp of pain from her.

Zach felt red hot anger roll over him. 'You hurt her and I'll …'

'You'll what, Hogan? Just remember that I'm the one holding the gun. Now move towards that wagon. I want that money.'

Zach moved very slowly, his every movement submissive so the man wouldn't make good his threat where Emily was concerned.

'Now light that lantern you've got hanging from the buckboard.'

Pulling a match from his shirt pocket Zach struck it across the buckboard's seat and lit the lamp, a sudden flare up of light being the result.

'That's better. Now I can see what you're up to. Now, slowly unbuckle your gun-belt and let it drop – and remember, you might be fast on the draw, but I've already got the hammer back on my shooting iron and the barrel's resting against your woman's head.'

Zach unbuckled the belt and let it drop.

'Now get in the wagon and get me that tin.'

As Zach clambered into the buckboard, the stranger lifted the lantern free and held it at the entrance to the canvas cover so he could keep an eye on Zach's doings. Only to do so meant he had to take his hand off Emily so he could grasp the light, just leaving the barrel of the pistol against her head courtesy of his gun hand.

Zach pulled the hay aside and picked up a tin.

'Bring it here!' the man charged him, his voice betraying his excitement.

Zach brought it over to the opening.

'Open it up, Hogan,' the man's voice was trembling with exhilaration.

Zach was no more than six feet from the fellow now, and so pulling the lid off the tin he reached inside, and pulling out the derringer he had put there for Emily's personal protection, swung it up and fired before the stranger even had time to react.

Zachariah Thompson's aim was good, which was fortunate, because if he had missed it would have been disastrous not only for him but for Emily as well. With a small hole punched neatly in the middle of his forehead, the hostage taker's pistol dropped from his grasp, clattering loudly on to the seat of the buckboard, bringing the hammer down and firing a bullet off into the dark night. The man stared straight at Zach, a look of utter bemusement on his face.

'Red Wilson is gunna have to wait a little longer for his money, it seems,' Zach said casually.

The mortally wounded man swayed slightly for a moment, his eyes widening noticeably as the bleeding in his brain intensified. With the lantern still firmly clutched in his left hand he suddenly toppled from the buckboard to crash heavily and loudly on to the ground beside the front wheel.

Emily sat down abruptly on the seat of the buckboard, all her courage spent. She had gone from fearing for her life and that of the man she loved, to witnessing the man who had created that fear dying right before her very eyes.

'It's all over now,' Zach said gently as he clambered out to join her. He placed an arm around her and pulled her in to him. 'There aren't any more of them.'

'Are you sure?' she asked with a trembling voice.

'Quite sure, there were only three horses following us, and I've dealt with three men, so we're safe now.'

'Will they send any more men after us?'

'Maybe, but by the time they catch up with us we'll already be in Helena. Folks there will vouch for me, I'm sure they will.'

The anguish seemed to melt away from her face. 'So can we travel at a more leisurely pace from now on?'

He smiled at her. It was the first time he had smiled in weeks. 'I don't see why not.'

She looked down at the man beneath her and shuddered. The lantern was still burning on the ground beside him where it had fallen, its light illuminating his features, horror-filled eyes set like stone in a pale face, drained of blood as a result of the small but deadly hole inflicted by the little bullet.

'What are we going to do with him and the other two?'

'I'll bury them in the morning. But now we must get some sleep. I'm afraid I haven't slept properly since we left Tombstone. But with this threat out of the way, I think I can allow myself the luxury of sleeping deeply at last.'

ELEVEN

After Zach had buried the three men he spent an hour catching their horses. They would be worth selling when they came to a town. So would the saddles, for that matter. He had rifled through the saddlebags and found nothing much of interest until he came to the last one. Pulling out a book he turned it over and read the title written on the cover out loud: *A Tale of Two Cities*. He chuckled, as the irony of it wasn't lost on him. 'Imagine one of those numbskulls reading great literature like that,' he said to himself.

He was about to slip it back, when on a whim he flipped it open and read an inscription inside the front cover. He froze. It was his book. But what stunned him most was what the inscription said: *This book belongs to the Reverend Zachariah Thompson, and was presented to him by his loving wife Sophia on their first wedding anniversary 1876.*

So not only was Zach a man of the cloth, but he was a married man as well. The revelation hit him hard. He had a wife out there somewhere, a wife who was probably thinking that because he had been gone so long, he was dead.

Then it dawned on him. The woman who had come to him in his dream, she must have been his wife, she must have been Sophia. But what he couldn't figure out was how Red Wilson's men had come by the book. That part just didn't make any sense to him at all.

He was going to have to tell Emily, and he knew she wasn't going to take it well. She had settled it in her mind that the two of them would be married once they had reached Helena and cleared up this case of mistaken identity. But with the revelation that he was a married man, that dream of hers just wasn't going to come to fruition, and no amount of tears was going to change that. No matter how gently he broke the news to her, she was still going to be devastated. He felt crushed enough about it himself. He couldn't even remember the woman who was supposed to be his wife. This *Sophia* was as much a stranger as those three men he had just buried. But Emily was real enough, and he had come to love her deeply, and so knowing she could not be his filled his heart with sorrow.

****

'I have something to tell you,' Zach said later on that morning as they trundled across an open stretch of ground, 'and I'm afraid it's something that's going to upset you.'

He noticed her body tense somewhat as she sat on the buckboard's seat beside him, her eyes staring off into the distance, not wishing for them to make contact with his until the worst was over.

'Go on,' she said quietly.

'I found a book in one of the saddlebags belonging to those men,' he gave the reins a gentle flick; the two horses were being particularly lazy this morning. 'The book was mine.'

She looked at him now, her green eyes searching his dark eyes for answers. 'How can that be?'

He shrugged his powerful shoulders. 'I have no idea. But that's not what is so upsetting.'

'There's more?'

He decided to launch right into it and just get it over with. 'The inscription in the book says it was given to me by a woman named Sophia. Apparently, Sophia is my wife.'

Emily's eyes closed, and she kept them closed. 'How can you be sure she is your wife?'

'Because it is written in the book that she is the wife of Zachariah Thompson. I'm sorry, Emily,' Zach said sincerely.

Emily swallowed hard. Her eyes were still tightly closed. 'How do you know that she is still alive?'

Zach hadn't thought about that. Sophia might very well be dead. That may be why he was here in Arizona instead of back in Montana. There was hope that he and Emily could be together yet. 'I don't know if she is still alive or not,' he conceded.

She opened her eyes then. 'I will not accept it until I know for certain you are still married, Zach. Until then my heart belongs to you.'

'We will clear this up when we get to Helena,' he promised. 'I'm sure Sophia must have passed on, or I wouldn't be here in Arizona without her.'

It made sense, or at least Emily wanted it to make sense. She couldn't bring herself to accept that he may never be hers, and so she was determined to push that possibility far from her thoughts. Zachariah Thompson was all the man she would ever need, he was all the man she would ever want, and she was sure that for as long as she lived, she would never meet another man she would love more.

Zach considered what lay ahead. Red Wilson wasn't likely to let things rest. But it would be a while before he discovered that his men had failed in the task he had sent them to do. Maybe he would trail Zach all the way to Helena. Thirty thousand dollars was a mighty big incentive. And of course, with several of his men now dead, that thirty thousand was going to be split a whole heap fewer ways than before. Red's share in it had just increased exponentially, and that in itself was motivation enough to keep hunting Zach down. So he might be forced to keep looking over his shoulder for a long time to come.

What puzzled him the most, and something he had withheld from Emily, was the revelation that he was a man of the cloth. Reverend Zachariah Thompson, the inscription had said. But although he could bring a few scripture verses to light, and knew the '*Our Father Who Art in Heaven*' psalm off by heart, he couldn't bring to mind any other passages in the bible, and that puzzled him. If being a minister of the Lord really was his occupation, then why couldn't he remember anything about what that job entailed? It just didn't add up.

He cast his mind back to last night's fracas. Where would a reverend have learnt to use a gun like he had? He instinctively knew how to use a gun, and not in the usual manner, but precisely how a professional gunman would. Was he a renegade reverend who had turned his back on his Lord? There were so many questions to which he craved the answers, but to which, sadly, he had none.

Really, everything hinged on making it back to Helena without either Red Wilson or the law preventing him from doing so. Surely the answers to all these questions lay waiting to be unveiled in that fair town, if only he could get there before anyone else got to him.

****

Zach didn't know when they had crossed over into Utah, possibly two or three days before, maybe even longer, but he *was* confident they were no longer in Arizona.

The supplies they had brought with them were all but gone now, and so it was with a certain amount of relief that a town loomed on the horizon one morning, as it would give them the opportunity to restock with essentials before they struck out for Montana again.

Cedar City is what the sign said the place was called as the buckboard neared the town, and Zach could see that it was a sizeable enough place to have everything they would need. He had hoped to stay away from towns that might boast their own law enforcement officers, but given the fact their supplies were severely depleted, and he had no idea how far it was to the next settlement that could answer their needs, he felt he really had no choice but to stop off here. Pulling his Stetson down over his eyes, and hunching over slightly, he steered the buckboard up Cedar City's main street.

'Can we stay a night here, Zach?' Emily asked. 'I would love to spend a night in a real bed for a change. I've slept on that pile of hay in the buckboard for so long I've almost forgotten what a mattress feels like. A bath would be good, too.'

He felt a stab of guilt. He had dragged her across country expecting her to suffer the same deprivations he had, not for one moment respecting the fact that she was not used to that kind of existence. Until the Apache had turned up that night at the Fawcett ranch she had been accustomed to a much more comfortable lifestyle. He owed her at least one night of comfort before they hit the trail again. 'Of course,' he said, and then smiled when she squealed in delight, and then throwing her arms around him, brazenly kissed him on his cheek.

Zach had to admit, as he lay in a tub full of hot water later on that afternoon, that Emily's idea to stop over till the next day had been a good one. With a fine cigar hanging out the corner of his mouth instead of his usual cheroot, he felt as content as a pig in mud.

He could do with a drink as well. He hadn't touched a drop of whiskey since leaving Tombstone, and now he was starting to crave the stuff. He chuckled to himself. He, a minister of the Lord, craving the devil's brew – how much further could a man slide? But dare he risk going into a saloon?

He could hear a hubbub of voices down on the street below, and figured everyone was too busy going about their own business to be concerned about any strangers who might turn up in town. Who would be expecting a gunfighter like Clint Hogan to turn up in a little town like Cedar City just out of the blue anyway? He would be all right, he was sure he would be. He would have a quick drink and then hightail it back to his lodgings before Emily even knew he was gone. Climbing out of the tub he hurriedly towelled himself down, and then putting on a clean set of clothes, headed downstairs. Emily would still be bathing, he figured, a woman always did take a lot longer over making herself presentable than a man did, and so he figured that what she didn't know couldn't possibly hurt her. With a raging thirst coming on he stepped out into the street, and, mixing in with the folks of Cedar City as they bustled along, went in search of a saloon.

'What can I get you, mister?' the man behind the bar at McClintock's Saloon asked Zach when he reached inside his jacket pocket for some money.

'Whiskey, and make it the very best you've got too, pard.'

The man grinned. 'You sound like a man who's been deprived for too long.'

'You don't know the half of it.'

'Well, I've got just what you need right here.' He turned around, and reaching up pulled a bottle down from a high shelf. 'This stuff'll make you realize what you've been missing out on all these years.'

'That good, huh?'

The cork came off and the bartender tipped a generous amount of the dark liquid into a glass, 'That and more, my friend, that and more.'

Zach put the glass to his lips. 'You weren't wrong,' he said when he had brought it down again.

'Haven't seen you around here before – are you intending on staying in Cedar City?'

Zach shook his head. 'I'm heading for Montana.'

'Got family there?'

'I hope so.'

'Haven't been back there in quite a while, I take it.'

'You could say that.' In fact, Zach had absolutely no idea the last time he had been in Montana. He knocked the rest of the whiskey back and pushed the glass towards the bartender for a refill.

'It's habit forming that stuff, ain't it?' The man's grin had widened.

'It sure is, and it's a habit I could easily get used to.'

'We had a little excitement in town yesterday,' the bartender said as he topped Zach's glass up for him. 'A couple of fellers stopped off right here in the saloon. They were flashing a lot of money around. I knew straight off they hadn't come by that money the honest way.'

'Oh?'

'No sirree, they had wads of the stuff, and they weren't afraid to splash it around. Nothing was too good for them. Ended up, they were wanted by the law.'

'You don't say.' Zach was only half listening, he was too intent on sampling this splendid whiskey.

'Someone recognized 'em and hightailed it to the sheriff's office. But by the time the sheriff got here the two hombres had vamoosed. One minute they was here, and the next minute they was gone. They musta got wind of it somehow. Anyway, I heard tell they was part of the Red Wilson gang.'

Zach Thompson sure heard that, and so he gave the bartender his full attention. 'The Red Wilson gang, you say?'

'Yep, it was Rex Tyrell and Chuck Harrison, so I was told. Word around town was Clint Hogan was supposed to be riding with them, but he wasn't with them when they came in here. They robbed thirty thousand dollars … thirty thousand, mind, from some bank, don't remember exactly where.'

Zach's heart sank. Of all the towns he could have chosen to stop off at, it had to be the one that Red Wilson's men had just been in. The law in Cedar City would be on high alert right about now, and he had walked smack bang into the middle of it all. Fitting the description of Clint Hogan as closely as he did wasn't going to do his chances of remaining incognito any good whatsoever – what rotten luck he seemed to have.

After the bartender had left him to serve someone else, he downed another whiskey and thought about what he had just been told. Maybe the real Clint Hogan was out there somewhere not too far away. Maybe he and the other two hadn't split that loot up, but were drifting from town to town here in Utah. It would help Zach out if Hogan *was* captured. Not only would the law no longer be interested in Zach, but once Red Wilson received word that his former partner in crime was behind bars, then he would call his men off from tracking down Zach as well.

He bent his elbow again, and another shot of whiskey cascaded down his throat to join the first couple that right at this moment were warming his stomach nicely. It might be best if he got out of here. Whoever it was who had recognized Harrison and Tyrell might be in this very room. Dang it, several men had left since he had arrived, and any one of them could be down at the sheriff's office right now, excitedly telling the sheriff that Clint Hogan was downing whiskey in McClintock's Saloon.

'You off so soon?' the bartender said as Zach placed some money on the counter to pay for the whiskey.

Zach kept his head lowered so the man couldn't see his eyes. 'Yep, I figure I'd best get an early night. I'm leaving town early in the morning.'

'The best of luck then,' the man said, as he scooped the money up off the counter and slipped it into the pocket on his apron.

Zach walked quickly. He had to if he wanted to get off this street where prying eyes were everywhere. If he could get back to his lodgings unseen, then he could send Emily down to the mercantile in the morning to buy what they needed, and then she could swing by the boarding house and pick him up on the way out of town. That way he could greatly lessen the chances of being recognized.

He had reached the boarding house, and even had his hand on the doorknob, when a man stepped out of the shadows at the far end of the porch, a shotgun was in his hands, and it was pointed straight at Zach.

'Clint Hogan ... I'm placing you under arrest!'

TWELVE

Zach's heart sank. Why had he been so foolish as to go down to that saloon? A few shots of whiskey weren't worth what he was going to go through now, no matter how good the whiskey had been.

'Drop that gun-belt, Hogan, and do it real gentle if you want to carry on breathing.'

Zach did as he was told, and then turned to face his captor.

'You have to be the dumbest hombre I've ever come across,' the man said as he stepped into the sunlight and Zach caught a glimpse of the badge he wore on his shirt. 'Tyrell and Harrison must have told you they had been recognized in town yesterday, and yet you still breezed in like you didn't have a care in the world.'

'I don't suppose it'd do any good if I was to tell you I'm not Clint Hogan,' Zach said hopefully, but realizing he had about a snowball's chance in hell of the sheriff believing him.

'You'd do well to just keep your mouth shut!' the sheriff snapped. 'You might have come here with a mighty big

119

reputation, but you ain't nothing but a lowdown dirty skunk as far as I'm concerned, and I'd put a bullet in you just as soon as I'd put one in a skunk, too.'

The feller was obviously a no-nonsense sort of sheriff, so Zach decided the best policy would be to do as he was told and just keep his mouth shut.

The sheriff jerked his head in the direction of the street. 'Get movin', you've got a date with a jail cell.'

Zach stepped down off the porch, and with the sheriff treading warily along behind him, made his way up the main street, fully aware of the excited looks he was getting from the citizens of Cedar City, who were enjoying the spectacle of their small-town sheriff getting the better of the notorious outlaw who went by the name of Clint Hogan.

'I've just done my chances of re-election a power of good,' Cedar City's sheriff said as he clanged the cell door shut on Zach. 'Folks around here are gunna think Thomas Hoyden's just the cat's whiskers when they hear I've single-handedly brought in Clint Hogan. Didn't need to fire a shot neither,' he chuckled at the thought of it.

'I'm delighted for you,' Zach said sarcastically, knowing he shouldn't be saying anything to harm his chances of getting out of here, but unable to hide his dislike of the man.

'You just shut that mouth of yours, or I'll shut it for you!'

'You'd have to come in here to do that, and I figure you ain't got the guts.' It was a long shot, but if Hoyden was foolish enough to open the door and take Zach on, then Zach would fight tooth and nail to overpower him and escape. He had no desire to wind up dangling at the end of a rope, and he fancied that was exactly what was going to happen to him if he didn't get out of here before he stood trial.

Sheriff Thomas Hoyden's face flushed with anger. 'You filthy gutter rat. I ought to shoot you on the spot and tell everyone you were trying to escape. But I'm not gunna do that because I want to see you squirmin' at the end of a noose.' Turning on his heel, he stormed out of the cell block and into his office, banging the heavy oak door between the two rooms shut as he went.

Well, that hadn't worked, and as Zach sat down on the flea-infested cot beneath the barred window, he pondered his fate. He didn't have a single friend in this town, no one who could verify that he wasn't Clint Hogan, and so his chances of being alive by this time next month were practically zero. He was going to need a miracle to get out of this one, and somehow, he couldn't see a miracle heading his way any time soon.

****

Zach slept fitfully that evening. The dream that had haunted him that night out on the trail came back with a vengeance. The tall man who stepped through the veil of gloom to stand over him peered down into Zach's face with icy-cold blue eyes that radiated malevolence, and even though Zach got a good look at the face, he still didn't know who the man was – although it was obvious the spectre wished nothing but harm to Zachariah Thompson.

The man's mouth opened, and Zach caught a glimpse of the tobacco-stained teeth and receding gums of his adversary. *'You betrayed me!'* The man unbuttoned his coat, and parting it, showed Zach the bloodied mass of torn flesh that lay beneath.

Zach woke with a start, his body cold and clammy to the touch, his heart racing uncontrollably. What did that man have to do with him?

Swinging his long legs over the side of the cot, he sat up, the full moon casting light across one side of his face as it streamed in through the barred window above him. His chest was heaving as he drew in the cool night air, all the while telling himself that it had only been a dream, no need to get so worked up about it.

He scratched his leg as he thought about what he had just seen. Although he hadn't recognized the man, he had been aware that the two of them were, or at least had been, acquainted at some time. But for the moment he just couldn't remember how or where.

His hand moved from his leg to his stomach to scratch an itch there. If only he could remember who the feller was, then maybe he could start putting the pieces of this puzzle together. He rubbed a spot under his arm and gazed down at the whiteness of the flagstones as they reflected the brilliance of the ancient globe. That moon sure was bright tonight.

Zach stood up suddenly – his entire body was itching. Pulling up his shirt, he examined his flesh in the glow of the moon, which revealed small red lumps liberally sprinkled across his torso. 'Dang fleas!' he muttered angrily, as the reason for his discomfort dawned on him. 'As if I haven't got enough to contend with as it is.' Dragging the mattress off the cot he banged it savagely against the stone walls of the cell several times in a desperate attempt to knock the fleas off. 'If nothing else, you'll all have king-size headaches, you little varmints,' he said, as he thumped the mattress back down on the cot again.

Before long, weariness overcame him, and so with the greatest of reluctance he lay back down on the mattress and trusted his dwindling blood supply to fate. Within minutes he had drifted off again, a victim of the exhaustion that the past few days had brought his way.

And then she was suddenly there again, her face just as pale as it had been the first time she had appeared to him, her auburn hair blowing around her head as if it was weathering a storm. He knew that face. That face had meant so much to him at one time. 'Sophia!' he shouted, 'is that you?'

A pained expression came over her face, and a tear slipped from the corner of her eye and slid down her pallid cheek. *'We could have been so happy together,'* she said. *'I didn't need money, I just needed you.'* She began to fade away, much as she had the first time she had visited him.

'Sophia … don't go, Sophia,' he pleaded. But it was too late: the young woman had been swallowed up by the same darkness that had exposed her to him.

He was awake, sitting on the edge of the cot again, his head in his hands. She was his wife, she had to be. She could be none other than the Sophia who had given him that edition of *A Tale of Two Cities*. What did she mean by not needing *money*? Did that have something to do with why she wasn't here with him now?

A loud noise behind him jolted him free of his musings. Someone was outside his cell window, and it sounded like they were trying to toss something between the bars.

There it was again – something small but metallic clanked against the bars of the window before dropping back again outside. He waited impatiently for it to happen again, but this time the object cleared the window and clattered noisily on to the stone floor of the cell.

Zach stared down at it as it glistened in the light of the moon. It was his old Colt .44, and it had a piece of rolled-up paper poking out of the barrel. Stooping down he picked the pistol up, and extracting the paper, smoothed it out so he could read it by the light that streamed in through the window.

It was from Emily. She would be waiting for him behind the jail with two saddled horses. The rest would be up to him. Pulling his fob watch from his pocket he popped it open: 2.35am, the perfect hour to attempt an escape. She must have found his six-gun and holster on the porch at the boarding house where he had been ordered to drop it, and then putting two and two together, figured out that he had been arrested. Emily had really come through for him this time.

'Sheriff!' he hollered. 'Sheriff Thomas Hoyden!'

There was a creaking of bedsprings out in the sheriff's office and a muffled curse, then the oak door swung open and the sheriff peered through. 'What in tarnation is going on in there?' he demanded.

'I need to see the doctor.'

'What for?'

'I'm bleeding … bleeding bad.'

'How in the blazes did you manage that?'

'It's this rusty old cot. The edge of it has got a jagged piece of steel sticking up. I went to get out of bed and tore my leg open on it. I'm bleeding like a stuck pig.'

'Can't it wait till the morning?'

'I'll be dead by then.'

'Nothing less than what you deserve. Besides, you're gunna be dead in a month or so anyways. The hangman's gunna see to that.'

'How you gunna explain my death to folks? It'll look like you used a knife on me and then just left me to bleed to death.'

Hoyden sighed. 'I'll get a lamp and take a look at it. If it looks bad enough then I'll go and get the doc. But I'm warning you, Hogan, you better not be wasting my time. I don't take kindly to having my sleep interrupted.'

While Hoyden went off in search of a lantern Zach pushed the Colt into the waistband at the back of his trousers and waited. If he messed this up then he was going to be dead for sure. Hoyden would put a bullet in him at the first sign of trouble.

A few minutes later the sheriff returned, his left hand clutching a dimly burning lantern that he was holding up at face level. 'Come over by the bars where I can get a look at that leg of yours,' he said gruffly.

As Zach reached the cell door he whipped his .44 out and pointed it at Hoyden through the bars. 'Do exactly as I tell you and I won't have to kill you!' he said fiercely.

'Dang it, Hogan, where'd you get that shooting iron?'

'Never you mind. You just lift the keys off the wall behind you and open this door.'

'The hell I will!'

Zach clicked back the hammer on the Colt. 'Have it your way, sheriff.' He brought the pistol up and aimed it at Hoyden's chest.

'All right, all right,' the sheriff said quickly, fearing Clint Hogan's reputation as a man who threw caution to the wind, 'I'll let you out. But I have to warn you that they'll come after you, and it won't be to take you prisoner. You'll be shot on sight.'

'I'll take my chances with that. Now, get those keys!'

Sheriff Hoyden did as he was told. He would have been foolish not to have. Clint Hogan with a gun in his hand was a force to be reckoned with, and Hoyden didn't fancy being the one doing the reckoning.

The keys jangled as the sheriff found the correct one, then within seconds the cell door was open, and Zach was through it in a jiffy. 'Sorry about this,' he said, as he brought the .44 down on Hoyden's head, knocking the man unconscious on the spot. Catching him before he hit the floor, Zach dragged him into the cell and dumped him on the cot. 'There you go, boys,' he said gleefully to whatever fleas still lurked in the musty old mattress, 'breakfast is served.'

Locking the cell door behind him, Zach quickly made his way out to the office and peeked out the door to make sure the street was clear. It was. Slipping through he made his way around to the back of the jail to where Emily was waiting with the horses.

'You're an angel sent straight down from heaven, Emily,' he said appreciatively, as he took the reins from her and mounted his mare.

'You didn't kill him, did you?' Emily asked nervously.

'No, I wouldn't do that. But I had to hit him over the head.'

'How long have we got before he sounds the alarm?'

'Three hours maybe.'

'Then we had better get moving,' she turned her mare's head towards the street, and without a moment's hesitation spurred her mount into action.

Zach Thompson grinned as he watched the young woman's back disappearing down the deserted street. 'You're quite some woman, Emily Fawcett,' he said quietly to himself, and then the thrill of being free brought a rush of blood to his head, and he moved off after her at a gallop.

THIRTEEN

Three days later, Zach was feeling confident they had given any posse from Cedar City the slip. They had avoided any settlements and were living off the provisions Emily had rustled up the night she had broken Zach out of jail. They had enough to keep them going for another week if they strictly rationed it. It would be water that would be the problem, especially for the two mares, and in this desert region they were travelling through now, water appeared to be rather a scarce commodity.

The horses got wind of water the next day. Sniffing the breeze they both whinnied loudly and tossed their heads in anticipation, then breaking into a trot, headed for the life-giving substance of which they had been given precious little for the past few days.

Zach and Emily gave them their heads. There was no point in struggling to keep them under control when their natural instincts were kicking in. They would have to make sure the horses didn't overdo it once they found the water hole, though. Zach had seen more than one horse die in the past from consuming too much water too quickly.

'Whoa,' Zach changed his mind the second he saw the two men up ahead. 'Rein your mare in, Emily,' he shouted.

With difficulty, Emily persuaded her mount to come to a standstill, but not without having to pull back on the bit harder than she would have liked to.

Zach surveyed the situation from his saddle. There were two men standing beside a water hole not more than one hundred and fifty yards away, their horses standing off to the side, nibbling at the brush that grew nearby.

'Are they dangerous?' Emily asked nervously.

'I don't know yet.' The problem was they needed that water. There might not be another hole for days, and the horses mightn't last that long. That clinched it for Zach. They would ride on in and take their chances that the two hombres were harmless. The alternative was dying of thirst, and that didn't bear thinking about.

Emily looked at him expectantly.

'Keep well to my left as we ride in, and keep your mare's head down so she doesn't pick it up faster than walking pace.'

She nodded.

'Let's see what we're up against.' Zach spurred his mare on, keeping his eyes on the two men the entire time.

As they got closer, Zach could see the two men had been living rough for some time. Unshaven for several months, and with faded and torn shirts, each man looked to be the epitome of a desperado.

Thirty yards out and Zach could see their eyes were trained on Emily. They obviously hadn't seen a woman in a while, and so they liked what they were seeing now. Zach would have to watch their gun hands the whole time if he didn't want Emily to fall victim to a pair of sexual deviants.

'Howdy,' Zach called out when he was close enough for easy conversation.

There was no answer, they just continued to watch Emily as she bobbed up and down in the saddle, and then one turned and said something to the other one before turning his face back and addressing Zach. 'I guess it'll be water you're wanting. There's plenty here for both you and your horses.'

It was a ruse. All Zach's instincts told him they were going to try and lull him into a false sense of security and then strike when he least expected it, Emily being their prize when they had disposed of Zach.

'You're welcome to camp here with us for the night if you want,' the fellow said in a genial manner, but Zach could tell that it was forced.

'We just want to water the horses and then we'll be on our way.'

'What's the hurry? Stay for a cup of coffee and a bite to eat.'

Zach couldn't see a campfire anywhere. He doubted these two had any coffee, and the only food they would have to offer would be the jerky they had been punishing their teeth with since they ran out of real food. Nope, these two hombres spelled trouble, and so Zach wasn't going to turn his back on them for as long as a single second.

He was close enough to get a good look at them now. Worse deadbeats than these two barrel-boarders a man could never hope to meet, and if first impressions were accurate, then Zach had just run across humanity's dregs way out here in the middle of nowhere.

The lecherous way they eyed Emily when the two mares were drawn up a few yards short of them left Zach in no doubt that his earlier estimation of them had been accurate. They would try to take her for their pleasure, and would leave Zach for dead the first opportunity they got.

'I take it the water is good?' Zach asked, his hand resting beside the butt of his Colt .44, and his eyes alert for the slightest movement on the part of either of the two men.

'Yep, we and our horses have been drinking it for the past three days and nothing has happened to us,' one of the men answered, and then tearing his eyes away from Emily looked Zach full in the face.

Zach saw instant shock register in the man's eyes.

'Hogan!' he rasped out. 'But you're dead!' His hand immediately snaked down to the six-gun on his hip.

Zach had been expecting as much, but not nearly so soon. Without missing a beat, his own hand closed on the old .44, and lifting it clear of its leather confines he thumbed back the hammer and brought his index finger down on the trigger.

The resultant explosion echoed across the flat rocky terrain, and hadn't died away before the hammer came back on the Colt again, and the second man succumbed to some hot lead in much the same way as the first one had, his pistol not quite clear of his holster. He might have had Zach in trouble if his eyes had been where they should have been, watching Zach, instead of on Emily. As it was, when his friend made his play, his attention had been completely diverted, and he had to play catch-up – but that was something you couldn't do and hope to stay alive when up against a gunman of Zach Thompson's calibre.

Emily could only look on in bewilderment as the two men lay in the red Utah dirt and took in their final breaths.

'I'm beginning to hate the name of Clint Hogan,' Zach said sombrely. 'It seems everywhere it goes death follows closely behind.'

'It's not your fault men keep trying to kill you,' Emily said, looking away from the grisly scene that threatened to make her vomit.

'Isn't it? I'm beginning to wonder. Maybe this Clint Hogan character and I are more alike than I've been giving it credit. I seem to be able to take a man's life at the drop of a hat, and that isn't normal for a preacher, now is it?'

She had to agree that it wasn't, even though she wasn't going to tell him that.

He got down from his mare and checked that both men were dead. They were, both men's hearts had been pierced, and it left Zach wondering how he had managed it. 'Let's water the horses,' he said as he straightened up. 'As soon as we've done that I'll bury these two out there somewhere.'

When she had turned away he noticed the pearl-handled Navy Colt that one of the men had dropped, and stooping down, he picked it up to inspect it. For some reason it felt vaguely familiar, as if he had seen it before, and he had to confess that it did feel real good in the palm of his hand, almost like it was made to order. Much better in fact, than the old .44 he had in his holster at the moment. The dead feller wouldn't need it anymore, so what was the harm in keeping it for himself? Slipping his .44 into the dead man's holster, Zach let the Navy Colt find a new home in his own.

****

Several hours later Zach placed the very last rock on top of the men's bodies. Without a shovel he had been able to do no more than scoop a shallow depression in the hard ground and roll the bodies into it. A generous pile of rocks stacked on top would prevent the wild critters from digging them up, as well as the stench of decay from escaping. When he got back to the waterhole Emily had nearly finished frying up a few cuts of ham over a fire she had kindled.

Zach walked over to the men's saddles that were lying under the shade of a juniper bush, and opening up the saddlebags on the first one, rummaged around inside it. There wasn't much of interest there – a plug of tobacco and a few coins were the sum total of that fellow's wealth. He turned his attention to the other saddlebag, and lifting the leather flap, peeked in, expecting similar contents to the first one. But he instantly flinched: it was crammed full of money, wads and wads of the stuff. He exacted a quick count. Why, there must be close to thirty thousand dollars in there.

And then the penny dropped. This was the money from the bank job that the Red Wilson gang had pulled off, the very same money that had been causing Zach so much trouble, the reason why so many people were out for his blood. Those two men he had just killed must have been none other than Tyrell and Harrison, the two hombres Hogan was supposed to have skedaddled with along with the loot – only Hogan hadn't been with them after all. Maybe those two snakes had disposed of him somewhere along the way so they could keep all the money for themselves. After all, one of them did say to Zach that he had thought he was dead.

Picking up the saddlebag that contained the loot, Zach walked over to the fire and dropped it at Emily's feet. 'This is what all the ballyhoo has been about.'

She looked at the bags and then at him with incomprehension in her eyes.

'Take a look inside, Emily.'

She lifted the flap and gasped.

'That's what thirty thousand dollars in cold hard cash looks like.'

'Is this the money that everyone thought you had?'

He nodded. 'Well, it's the money everyone thought Clint Hogan had.'

'And those two?' she nodded off in the direction Zach had just buried them.

'Red Wilson's men. I figure they killed Hogan and high-tailed it with the money. They were probably afraid of

Hogan and his reputation as a fast gun and so decided it was safer to put a bullet in him when his back was turned.'

'No honour amongst thieves, you mean?'

'I couldn't have put it better myself.'

'So what are we going to do with all this money?'

'There's plenty of things I could do with it.'

She looked shocked. 'Zach ... you're not thinking of keeping it, are you?'

'Why not, we haven't stolen it. We've merely found it.'

'That doesn't make it right. We need to get it back to the bank where it was stolen from, or at least to a sheriff's office somewhere so they can return it.'

'And risk placing my neck in the hangman's noose? Look what happened to me back in Cedar City. No fear, I'm not going to place myself in danger like that again.'

'But Zach, it isn't right.'

Zach scowled at her. He couldn't see what was wrong with keeping it. After all, the wretched stuff had been the cause of all his woes these past few months, so as far as he was concerned he was entitled to every last dollar of it, to compensate him for the hell he had been put through.

'No, Zach,' she said firmly.

He sighed. 'Then what do you suggest we do with it, Emily?' he asked gruffly.

'I could drop it off at the sheriff's office in the next town we come to. I'll put a note inside with the money explaining it's from the bank job the Red Wilson gang pulled, and that I found it in the possession of two dead men. Maybe that'll be enough to stop the law from hunting for you.'

Zach doubted it. The law wouldn't rest until they had captured Clint Hogan, and that probably wouldn't happen now if Harrison and Tyrell really had killed him, and so everywhere Zach went he was going to be at risk, at least until he reached Helena. 'I don't know how safe it would be for you to return this money,' he said lamely.

'Zachariah Thompson, we are returning this money to its rightful owners whether you like it or not!' she said adamantly.

He grinned at her, knowing that she had him beat. 'All right, your royal highness, we'll do the right thing and return the money, just as soon as it's safe enough to do so.'

Zach slept soundly that night, miles away from civilization and heartily glad of it. The horses were well watered, he and Emily were well fed, the millions of stars that twinkled brightly in the clear desert sky provided the best entertainment he had seen in years, and he fancied it wouldn't be too long before they crossed over into Montana – and of course with that would come the affidavits from the good folks of Helena, who would vouch for him being just plain old Zachariah Thompson instead of the hardened killer Clint Hogan. Yep, he wasn't too far away from snuffing out the terrible consequences of mistaken identity that had dogged him for the past few months, and he would soon be able to resume his life … whatever that proved to be.

FOURTEEN

There were no more incidents for Zach and Emily as they crossed Utah and then on up into Idaho. And Emily even got to keep her word, waiting for the sheriff of Eagle Rock to step out of his office for a while so she could drop the saddlebags, along with a note, on his desk. She chuckled to herself as she thought about the surprise he would get when he opened up those saddlebags and saw thirty thousand dollars in cash staring back at him.

Before she left town she bought a buckboard and sturdy canvas off the livery man to replace the wagon they had been forced to leave behind in Cedar City.

'How far is it to Helena now?' Emily asked a few weeks later as she shifted her weight to try and ease the sores that the wooden seat of the buckboard had fashioned on her backside.

'I think it can't be more than a week to ten days away now,' Zach confided. He knew they had crossed over into Montana a few days ago. Everything about the terrain screamed out Montana, good cattle country that it was, and so he felt his spirits lifting as he sensed that his quest to clear his name wasn't too far away from being fulfilled.

That night as he bedded down under the stars he fully expected to sleep the sleep of a contented man, just as he had done so every night since he had left the waterhole in Utah behind. But Zach Thompson was in for a nasty surprise, and it would be one that would shake him to the core – and what was more, he wouldn't receive it from the living, but that surprise was about to come to him from the dead.

He had been sound asleep for six hours or so when she came to him. She was the same woman who had haunted his dreams on two other occasions: the woman he had assumed was his wife Sophia.

As her face swam into focus he heard himself calling out her name: 'Sophia, it's me!' he shouted.

Her eyebrows came down in consternation. 'It's Laura ... it's Laura ... it's Laura,' she sang back to him, making the hair on the back of his neck stand up on end as she floated closer to him.

The name struck a chord. Laura ... yes, he remembered her now. She had been his wife once, and he had loved her more than anything.

'I told you not to do it,' she said mournfully, as she hovered just above his face, 'but you would not listen. I am dead because of what you did, and now you must learn to live without me.'

'I'm sorry, Laura,' he sobbed, the tears forming in his eyes beginning to obstruct his view of her. 'I never meant for you to get hurt.'

'That is over now. I cannot come to you again, but one day you may come to me. Until then you must live as I asked you to, or we shall be lost to each other forever. You must promise me.'

'I promise, Laura, I promise to live as you asked me to.'

She smiled at him then, and began to fade from view.

'Come back, Laura,' he pleaded, 'come back. There is so much I want to say to you.' But she was gone, and in his heart he knew he would never see her again in this world.

Seconds passed, and just when he thought his heart would explode from the grief, the second spectre visited him.

'Not you again!' Zach rasped throatily as the older man appeared from behind the same shadowy veil Laura had been swallowed up by.

'You betrayed me!' the wretch said as he drifted towards Zach.

'I don't even know you,' Zach protested.

'You knew me for a brief moment in time,' the ghoul insisted. 'My life was in your hands and I trusted you to keep it safe. But you betrayed me into the hands of others.'

'I don't know what you mean,' Zach cried out.

'You let them kill me. You promised me you would keep me safe, but you turned your back on me when I needed you most. My blood is on your hands.' He opened up his jacket to show Zach that same bloody wound that had so appalled Zach the first time, forcing the young man to look at it. 'This is what they did to me.'

'I'm sorry … I'm sorry … but I just don't remember,' Zach cried out.

'It is my wife who has suffered the most. It is she who must go on without me. It is you who must see that she is provided for.'

'I will ... just tell me who she is,' but he was fading fast, and Zach knew that just like Laura before him, he couldn't hold on to this world any longer.

That was when Zachariah Thompson woke up, his head throbbing and his throat dry. His hand went up to probe the wound that had caused his memory loss, and although he could feel that it had completely healed, still it hurt like it had only just been inflicted. Scrabbling off his bedroll he staggered down to the little creek below the campsite, and squatting down splashed the cold water onto his face and neck.

It had been a dream. A horrible nightmare that had brought the pain of his head wound on again. But at least the chilling water was bringing him a small measure of comfort.

As the water soothed him, his tired brain began to kick into gear, and one by one little pieces of his hidden memories started coming back to him.

Laura had been his wife. He hadn't been married to Sophia at all. He had no idea who Sophia even was. Her name had been written in his copy of that book, but she hadn't been his wife like she had claimed she was. No, Laura had been his wife, he remembered that clearly now.

Yes, things were coming back to him, slowly at first, but gathering in momentum until they were rushing in upon him like a flood. He cradled his head in his hands. 'No... no... no!' he screamed, as the terrible truth began to dawn on him.

Emily abandoned her repose in the wagon the moment she heard his agonized shrieks, and with the dawn's early light just starting to kiss the ground all around the campsite, she ran down to the creek to see what the matter was.

'Zach … are you all right?' she asked fearfully.

'I'm him … I'm him,' Zach said hysterically.

'Zach, tell me what's wrong,' she begged.

'I'm him … oh, God, please help me.' He looked at her through half-crazed eyes. 'I'm him!'

Emily was beginning to feel uncomfortable now. She had never seen him behave this way. 'You're who?' she asked.

'I'm him … I'm Clint Hogan.'

She stared at him in disbelief. 'Zach, what are you talking about?'

'It's all coming back to me, Emily. I'm Clint Hogan. I'm a cold-blooded killer.'

'No,' she moved towards him in an attempt to comfort him. 'You're Zach Thompson, it says so in your bible.'

'That's not my bible. That's his bible.'

'Clint Hogan?'

'No, Zachariah Thompson. That bible was his.'

'Zach, none of this is making any sense to me.' She placed her hand upon his shoulder and discovered he was trembling, and not because it was a cold morning.

'I am not Zachariah Thompson,' he said emphatically. 'I am Clint Hogan.'

She pulled her hand away. 'You're starting to frighten me, Zach.'

'You should be frightened. I'm not a good man, Emily. I've done things that no man ever should.'

She couldn't believe it. She wouldn't believe it. The man standing before her was a kind man, a decent man, and he would only harm another if either his life or the life of a loved one was threatened. No, there must be some mistake. This man was not an outlaw. He was not Clint Hogan.

'That woman Sophia, whose name was written in the bible … she was Zach Thompson's wife, not mine.' He was rambling now, letting it all flow out of him. It had been hidden for so long that he felt he had to get it out for the world to see. 'My wife's name is Laura. I remember her now. She was beautiful, and I let her down. She would still be alive if it wasn't for me.'

Although what he was saying terrified her, Emily knew she had to be brave, if only for his sake. 'Are you sure you are Clint Hogan?'

He nodded. 'It's all coming back to me now. I wish I wasn't him, but I am.'

It made sense to her. It would be why he kept getting recognized as the notorious gunfighter, and because he had received such a serious head wound he had lost all recollection of his true identity. Until now, that was.

'But why did you have that bible in your saddlebags if it didn't belong to you?'

Zach hung his head in shame. 'Zachariah Thompson was a preacher we took as a hostage after we robbed the bank in Helena. He had that bible in his saddlebags.'

'Where is he now?'

'Dead, and I'm responsible for it.' He could see the incomprehension in her eyes, so elaborated. 'We hit the bank in Helena, and the preacher happened to be in there at the time. We took him hostage so we could get out of town without being shot at, and it worked. Only a few miles out of Helena, Tyrell pulled out a shotgun and blasted the old man in the chest with it.'

'So how does that make you responsible?'

'When we took the old man I gave him my word that I wouldn't let the others harm him, and I fully intended to keep my word to him. But Red gave me orders to watch our back trail to make sure we weren't being followed, and although the old man begged me not to leave him alone with the rest of the gang, I did as Red told me. After I'd made sure we weren't being followed, I rode to catch up with the others and found Thompson dead by the side of the road. Tyrell had taken Thompson's horse and left his own lame one behind.'

'Why couldn't he have just let the old man go?'

Zach's face clouded over with fury. 'Because he was scum, and he cared for nobody but himself. An old man like Zachariah Thompson didn't mean anything to him, and Tyrell enjoyed inflicting pain on others. Watching him die would have brought him pleasure.' The memory of finding the old man and the guilt he had felt over it came rushing back to him. He tried to stifle the tears but they came on regardless.

Rushing to him, Emily took him into her arms in an attempt to comfort him. 'I'm sure the old man wouldn't blame you for what happened.'

'Oh yes, he does,' Zach said adamantly, the dream he had just had still fresh in his mind. 'He blames me for it all.'

She didn't argue with him. It was best to just leave him be to try and come to terms with everything that had happened. He had been given a tremendous shock – he wasn't the man he had thought he was, and he didn't like the man he now knew himself to be. That was enough to play havoc with any man's frame of mind.

'Laura blames me too.'

'Your wife?'

'Her family never wanted her to marry me. They were well-to-do, and I was from humble origins. They knew I would never amount to anything, and they were right. I could barely find enough work to keep the two of us. I was good with a gun, and so won money from time to time in organized shooting contests, but I knew I could never make a living at it.'

She guessed the rest. 'So you fell in with the Red Wilson gang to get your hands on enough money?'

'It was the only way I could get a large amount of money quickly. Red approached me because of my reputation with a gun, which up until then had only been used for legal purposes, and offered to make me rich if I threw in my lot with him. I planned to do a few bank jobs and then buy a business with the proceeds. I was determined to show Laura's family that I could keep her in the style to which she had been accustomed.'

'So what happened?'

'She begged me not to turn to crime. She assured me she didn't care about money. She said she just wanted me. But I was a proud man and had made up my mind that she would have everything she had had before we were married, and so when Red invited me to go along with them on a bank job, I did. That was six years ago now – I was twenty-two years old at the time.'

'How did she die?'

His expression became glummer than ever. 'I became a wanted man on account of being part of the Red Wilson gang. That meant there was a reward on my head. When there's a reward on your head, bounty hunters come after you.'

'And one of them caught up with you?'

'He did, in Carson City. I was wanted dead or alive, and he seemed to prefer it being dead. He started firing at me in the street one day and so I fired back and killed him. But not before Laura had been hit by one of his bullets. She died right there in my arms. That was three years ago now, but it still seems like it was only yesterday to me.'

He broke down and cried like a little boy then, and it was obvious to Emily that he had loved Laura very much, and that the pain of having been the cause of her death was more than he could handle. She walked him back up to the camp, and sitting him down with his back against the wagon, let him cry himself out.

Later on, they ate breakfast in silence, the only sound to disturb the peace of the Montana morning being the chuckling of the little creek, as its cool waters travelled over and around the many rocks that adorned its bottom. With breakfast over, Zach quietly went about the business of getting the horses hooked to the wagon for the ride ahead. There was no point in going to Helena for the purpose of proving he was Zachariah Thompson any more, for the simple reason that he wasn't. But Thompson's widow still lived there, and so he was determined to make sure she would be cared for in her old age, despite the possibility it might result in his capture and execution. If he could find her and give her enough money to see her right, then it would go some way towards easing his guilt-ridden conscience.

'I need to tell you how all this came about,' Zach said to Emily as they rode along in the buckboard together later that day.

'I've been hoping you would,' she confessed.

'After we robbed the bank in Helena, and after Tyrell had murdered Zachariah Thompson, we got surprised by a posse about six or seven miles out of town. They must have ridden hard to catch up with us, 'cos we were riding like the devil was after us ourselves. Anyway, we were forced to split up.'

'And you were the one carrying the money?' She knew he must have been, because that's why Red Wilson had sent men after him.

'Yep, I was the feller the bank teller handed the sack of money to, because I was the only one of the gang Red trusted to play fair with it, and so because we hadn't got far enough away from Helena to share the loot out, I was still carrying it when that posse happened upon us.'

She was puzzled about something. 'How did you come to be in Arizona when the bank you robbed was in Montana?'

'That was where we had our hideout. We operated out of
the wilds of Arizona. We had a cabin there in a well-watered
canyon. But we had hit so many of the banks around Arizona,
Colorado and Nevada that we could hardly ride into any of
their towns without being instantly recognized. Red decided
that if we hit Helena no one would link it to us, seeing as they
hadn't heard of us up that way, it being so far off and all, and
so we decided we would split the money up and make our way
back to Arizona separately. That wouldn't attract anyone's
attention, cos they'd be looking for a gang, not lone drifters.

'But one of the bank tellers had seen a wanted poster of
Red when he had been visiting his brother in Tucson, and
recognized him instantly. He's a very distinctive-looking
feller, with that red hair of his. The teller shouted out his
name when Red stuck a gun in his face. He was lucky Red
didn't shoot him on the spot. That's how the law in Cedar
City knew it was me who'd been involved in that bank job,
'cos the authorities in Arizona knew I rode with the Red
Wilson gang, and when word of the bank job filtered down
that way they must have wired most everywhere they could
think of to let them know it was us who had done it, and to
be on the lookout for us.'

'If you all got separated early on, then how did Tyrell
and Harrison get their hands on the money?'

'I made it all the way back to Arizona on my own without incident. But about sixty miles from the hideout who
should I ride over a rise and bump into but ...'

'Tyrell and Harrison!' Emily said triumphantly. 'And
that's when they took the money off you.'

'It wasn't quite that simple. I wouldn't have just handed it over to them. I had never trusted Tyrell as it was.'

'Then how did they end up with it?'

'Because we were so close to the hideout we rode along together for a while until the horse Tyrell had killed Zachariah Thompson for pulled up lame. While he was checking out the animal's hoof I decided to get down off my mare and check her over, just to make sure she was holding up all right, as she had been ridden mighty hard and I was worried about her.'

His eyebrows came down to form a frown as he remembered back. 'I should have known never to turn my back on a snake like Tyrell. While I was bent over I felt a crushing blow on the back of my head. I remember everything going black as I fell, and then another blow to my head again, and then nothing after that. I figure he must have thought I was dead, or he would have put a bullet in me to finish me off. He and Harrison never went back to the hideout where we had all agreed to meet. They obviously decided to keep all the money for themselves. When I did come round I figured I'd been lying there for a day or so. Thompson's mare was there, lame of course, and when I looked in the saddlebags I found his bible and mistakenly thought I was Zachariah Thompson.' He looked at her with sadness in his eyes. 'I only wish that I was.'

'And the book you found in those saddlebags the night those men attacked our wagon, the one with the name *Sophia* in it, how did that get there?'

He smiled grimly. 'Tyrell found it in Thompson's saddlebags after we left Helena, that was before the posse surprised us, and he gave it to Harrison. That's one of the men I had to kill back at the waterhole. That feller always had his nose in a book. He wasn't interested when Tyrell offered him the bible, though. He reckoned it held no interest for him. That's why it was still in the saddlebags of the horse I was riding when your Pa found me.'

She sighed. 'It was that book that made you think you were still married. That's what's made you be so careful around me.'

He smiled at her then, knowing what was going through her mind. 'Just as well I did. If we'd got married at one of the towns we've passed through you'd be married to Clint Hogan by now, and that wouldn't have brought you any happiness, I can assure you of that.'

'I love you, Zach, and I don't care what your past has been.'

'I'm not Zach,' he reminded her. 'My name is Clint … Clint Hogan, so there can be no future for us, Emily.'

She looked lovingly into his eyes, and it was as if she hadn't heard. 'You will always be Zach to me.'

FIFTEEN

'Emily,' he began hesitantly, 'I have a very big favour to ask of you.'

She had been busily packing their things away in the buckboard as today was the day they would finally reach Helena. She stopped what she was doing and gave him her full attention.

He lowered his eyes so he wouldn't be looking directly into hers. 'I was wondering if I could borrow some of the money you were paid for your pa's ranch.'

'Of course, if we are going to be together then that money is yours too.'

He didn't tell her that they wouldn't be together after they had left Helena. There was no point in distressing her before he got this business with Thompson's widow over with. 'I will pay you back, although it may take me a while to do it.' He would get a job doing something, he didn't know what yet, but he would find something. It would take a long time to pay off what he planned on borrowing, years in fact, but he would pay it back, every last cent of it.

'How much do you need, Zach?'

'Two thousand dollars,' he saw the surprise in her eyes, and was straightaway worried that she was thinking he was trying to cheat her out of her inheritance. 'I want it to give to Sophia Thompson,' he explained. 'That way she won't be scrimping for money in the last years of her life.'

She nodded. 'Yes, something should be done for her. I'll make sure you get the money when we get to Helena.'

Zach couldn't tell whether she was disappointed in him or not. He hoped that she wasn't. If there was one person in his life whom he desperately hoped would never think ill of him it was Emily Fawcett.

'I'm wondering how I'm going to head into Helena without being recognized. It seems that so far everyone and his dog knows what Clint Hogan looks like. And it was only four months or so ago I helped rob the bank there.'

Emily took him in from head to foot. 'You aren't the same man you were when you robbed that bank, Zach.'

He stiffened slightly, wondering whether she had gone off him enough to sling a putdown his way. 'What do you mean by that?'

'You haven't shaved since we left Tombstone. You have a full beard now, which you didn't have when Pa found you. You lost a stone or more in weight when we were nursing you, and you've lost another stone since we've been on the trail. What's more, those clothes you're wearing are all tattered and faded. I don't think anyone is going to believe you're Clint Hogan looking the way you do at the moment.'

Her description of him stung a little, but he guessed she was right. He was merely a shadow of the man he was when he had helped rob that bank several months back. But then, that would only work to his advantage.

He helped her up into the wagon when the time came to pull out. He wasn't sure what he was going to tell Sophia Thompson when he came face to face with her. Not the truth that was for sure. Not unless he wanted her running to the law and telling them Clint Hogan was in town. But he figured he could come up with something plausible by the time he found himself knocking on her front door and handing over two thousand dollars.

Several miles from town he could feel his pulse quicken. Just around the bend up ahead was where he had found Zachariah Thompson's body, and the nauseating sight of his belly ripped open by buckshot made him sick just thinking about it. He would do his best to look at the other side of the road when they passed by that particular spot.

'We need to talk about what is going to happen with us after you've done what you need to do in Helena,' Emily said, staring off into the distance as if she feared his answer wasn't going to be to her liking.

'Let's talk about that after I've got this out of the way.'

She turned to look at him now, and he fancied he saw a tinge of anger in her eyes. 'No, Zach, we'll talk about it now.'

He sighed. 'All right, have it your way.'

'Seeing as you are a widower, and no longer married like you thought you were, does that mean you're going to marry me?'

She had boxed him into a corner now, and he had to either lie to her to keep her happy for now, or he had to tell her the truth and make her miserable. After a few seconds thought, he decided on the latter. 'No, Emily, I'm not going to marry you. I'm an outlaw, and there is a warrant out for my arrest. That means I'm going to be forever on the run. I can't ask you to live that kind of a life.'

'Who said anything about you having to ask me? Shouldn't it be my decision as to whether I go on the run with you or not? Besides, I've been giving the matter some thought, and I've come up with an idea.'

The spot in the road where old man Thompson was brutally slain loomed up before them and so he twisted around on the seat and looked directly into Emily's eyes so he wouldn't have to see it up close. 'Go on,' he said, 'I'm listening.'

'We aren't too far from Canada, Zach. When we've concluded our business in Helena, why don't we just keep on going and cross over the border. You aren't a wanted man there, so we can get married and have a life together.'

He stared at her in mute silence for a moment or two. The idea actually had some merit. And he fancied they wouldn't have to travel too far into Canada to come to some place where they hadn't even heard of Clint Hogan. 'All right,' he said suddenly. 'But only if you think you can forget my past.'

'I won't have any trouble doing that, Zach, but what worries me is can *you* forget it?'

She had raised a good point, a point that at the moment he didn't know the answer to. He sure hoped he could forget, and if there was anyone who *could* help him to forget his past, then it would be her.

****

They arrived in Helena a while later, and given that the last time he had been here he had been on the wrong side of the law, he kept his head down and made sure not to make eye contact with anyone.

After getting the two thousand dollars together, Emily made enquiries as to how to get in touch with the widow Thompson; then armed with the necessary information, the pair sought out the little cottage with red roses spilling over a picket fence, and were soon knocking on the door.

A woman in her early sixties eventually answered, and peered out at them with the saddest of faces.

'Mrs Thompson?' Zach asked.

'Yes, I am Mrs Thompson,' she said, her sad eyes taking on a confused look. She obviously didn't get many visitors, and was struggling to figure out what a couple of strangers were doing calling on her.

'I am an acquaintance of your late husband,' Zach said. 'While he was alive he asked me to call on you in the event of his death. Would it be all right if my wife and I came in and spoke to you for a moment?'

As she opened the door to let them in, he could tell she was wondering how her lately departed husband could possibly have had anything to do with the uncouth-looking fellow standing in front of her now.

'Come through to the parlour,' Sophia Thompson said politely, and then led them through. 'In what way were you connected with my husband?' she asked Zach when they were all comfortably seated.

'Your husband was a great influence on me, Mrs Thompson. You might say he helped me to see the error of my ways.' He wasn't exactly lying, either. The way Zachariah Thompson had met his fate had made Zach sick to his stomach, and had made him want to leave his life of crime far behind. His coming to Zach in his dreams had prompted the younger man to do what he was doing now. So the reverend had indeed been a great influence.

For the first time she smiled. She was an attractive woman for her age, and Zach could only hope that her good looks might bring another man calling one day who would share what was left of her life with her. He hated the thought of her being all alone because of something he had done.

'My Zachariah helped a lot of people see the error of their ways,' she said proudly. 'He was murdered you know, on the road just a few miles out of town.'

Guilt swept over Zach in one gigantic wave. 'Yes, I had heard, Mrs Thompson, and that is why I'm here.' Reaching inside his jacket he pulled out an envelope containing the two thousand dollars and handed it to her. 'He wanted me to give you this.' Once again, he hadn't lied, because the spectre, if that was what he had been – or maybe it had been Zach's guilty mind conjuring up the ghost of Zachariah Thompson, either way it didn't matter – had wanted Zach to take care of Sophia, and so Zach was doing just that.

Sophia Thompson opened the envelope and looked inside. 'Why, I've never seen so much money in all my life. Where did it come from?'

'It came from your husband. He made provision for you, and asked me to deliver it to you if something should happen to him.' A stretching of the truth this time, but in a way the old man *had* made provision for her by prompting Zach to do what he was doing now.

'I was beginning to think that my final days on earth were going to be lived in poverty,' she said. 'But this will be more than enough to see me through.'

****

After they had left and taken on provisions for their journey to Canada, Zach felt a huge burden lift as the outskirts of Helena were rapidly left behind by the wheels of the buckboard. He could never atone for the harm he had caused, but at least he could be a force for good from now on. He looked down at the pearl-handled Navy Colt on his hip, the one Tyrell had stolen from him when he had left him for dead, but which Zach had found again in the man's possession at the waterhole in Utah, and hoped he would never have to use it to kill a man again.

They were ten miles out of Helena when two men rode out of a grove of trees and blocked the road in front of them. One was an Apache whom Zach had never seen before in his life, but the other was one he wished he never had. Handing the reins to Emily he stood up and with his hand resting beside the butt of his Navy Colt, waited patiently as the men slowly approached.

'You've been a hard man to run down, Clint,' the white man said. 'If it wasn't for this feller here being such a good tracker,' he jacked his thumb in the direction of his companion, 'I reckon you would have got away with it.'

'I don't want any trouble, Red,' Zach said edgily, his eyes on the gun hand of Red Wilson as he spoke.

'You should have thought of that before you ran off with my money.'

'Tyrell and Harrison took that money, Red. They left me for dead. If it wasn't for the woman sitting beside me nursing me back to life, then I would be dead by now.'

'Pity she wasted her time, Clint, because your reprieve is gunna be short-lived.'

'There's no need for this, Red.'

'I want my money, Clint, and I aim to have it.'

'It's gone.'

'What do you mean by *gone*. Surely you couldn't have spent all of it already.'

'I handed it in to the law.'

Red Wilson studied Clint's expression for a moment before grinning. 'You always were a kidder, Clint.'

Zach shook his head. 'This is one time I ain't kidding, Red. That money was returned to those we stole it off.'

'Now that makes me mighty disappointed in you, Clint. 'Cos either you're just plain stupid for giving it back, or you're lyin' to me so you can keep it all for yourself. Either way, it doesn't paint you in a good light with me.'

'Well, that's the way it is, so you'll just have to accept it.'

The grin on Wilson's face broadened. 'Do you know something, Clint, I always did wonder which of the two of us was the fastest, and I guess now we're gunna find out.'

Red Wilson's hand moved *so* fast that Zach wasn't quite sure whether he had the measure of him or not. Wilson's Remington was clear of its holster and pointing in Zach's direction right about the time Zach's Navy Colt was pointing in his. Two shots rang out loud and clear in the still morning air, one from each six-gun. But only one bullet struck its mark. Wilson sat there in his saddle staring back at Zach for what seemed like an eternity, his tall, statuesque frame unmoving, framed as it were by the verdant green of the trees beside the bend in the road behind him. His Remington slipped from his fingers, hitting his palomino on its front leg as it fell. As the gelding suddenly stepped back in fright, Wilson lurched back in the saddle, his head tilted upwards and his eyes staring in astonishment at the blue sky above him. He had just met his match, something he never thought would happen, not even against a gunman with the reputation of Clint Hogan, and all that remained for him to do now, was to plead his case before his Creator.

Clint didn't see Wilson slide from the saddle and thump heavily on the dirt road: he had already swung his Colt over to cover the Apache. 'What's it to be?' he demanded. 'Do you want to end up like him, or do you want to live?'

The Apache smiled calmly. 'He paid me to track you, not kill you. I have done my job.'

'Then we will not part enemies,' Zach said quietly, and with a jerk of his head indicated to the fellow that he could leave.

'What are you going to do with Red?' Emily asked, after the Apache had ridden off.

'Leave him here for someone to find. They'll get a pleasant surprise when they take him into town and find out there's a bounty on his head. They'll be a whole heap richer for it. At least that skunk'll end up being useful for once.' He sat down and taking the reins from her was about to guide the buckboard around Wilson's corpse when Emily placed her hand on his forearm to stop him.

Twisting around in his seat to get a better look at her he discovered she was smiling. 'What's got you looking so dang happy all of a sudden, ma'am?' he asked light-heartedly.

'I've just realized there's no one left to come after you.'

She was right. Wilson was dead, and the law wouldn't search for him in Canada. They were finally free.

She placed her hand against his cheek. 'We need a name for you. I want to keep calling you Zach because that's who you are to me now. But we need a surname to go with it.'

He smiled gently at her. 'What's wrong with Fawcett?'

'Oh, Zach,' her eyes misted over, 'Pa would have liked that. Any children we have will carry on his name.'

'Zach Fawcett it is then.'

'And what do you think we will do in Canada to keep mind, body, and soul together, Mr Fawcett?' she asked happily, not really caring what they would do, just so long as they did it together.

'We are young, strong and healthy, and we still have most of the money from the sale of the ranch. I'd say we can do just about whatever we dang well like.'

'Do you know what I'd like you to do right now, Zach?'

He shook his head.

'I'd like you to take me in your arms. I think I've waited long enough as it is for you to kiss me.'

A husky chuckle escaped his throat. 'I think that's something I can oblige you with, ma'am,' he said, and then with the gentleness that would be the trademark of Zachariah Fawcett for the rest of his life, he drew her in to him, and with the eagerness of a young man, kissed his future wife with overwhelming passion.